Jean Pierre Labaguette

for

US President

By

Richard Clement

Dedication

To all the healthy eaters and cynical voters...

Acknowledgment

Culinary arts and politics can have significant and lasting impacts. A bad cook, who leaves a bitter taste and causes indigestion, is likened to incompetent and corrupt politicians who create long-lasting chaos. The analogy extends to the idea that an improper diet leading to diseases and early death is similar to the consequences of ineffective governance. A talented French cook becomes US president and wants to make too many changes...

The author's wish for readers, is one day for them to be able to vote for a smarter presidency. This implies a belief that replacing human politicians with artificial intelligence could lead to a better and more stable planet.

This perspective reflects a view on the potential benefits of technology and artificial intelligence in governance, possibly as a means to reduce corruption, inefficiency, and long-term negative consequences in the political landscape. It's an exciting take on the intersection between food, technology and politics with a humorous twist about France and the USA.

Table of Contents

About The Author

Richard Clément, a French doctor and author, boasts a literary repertoire that includes three compelling books: "Latin Fiancée Visa," "The South African Virus Conspiracy," and "Jean Pierre Labaguette US President." With a penchant for exploration, he has traversed the landscapes of eighty-four countries, immersing himself in diverse cultures and cherishing the vibrant tapestry of life.

Embracing the ebb and flow of existence, Richard Clément astutely acknowledges the myriad facets of life's journey— a narrative interwoven with both poignant tragedies and delightful anecdotes. In his perceptive view, politics embodies a fascinating blend of tragedy and comedy, mirroring the intricate complexities and inherent contradictions present in social situations.

Having embraced American citizenship, Dr. Richard Clément has chosen Miami as his abode, where he passionately dedicates his time to crafting a cinematic masterpiece based on his inaugural literary work, "Latin Fiancée Visa." The film, aptly titled "Sex, Salsa, and Scams," promises to captivate audiences with its exploration of love, culture, and the intriguing world of visa intricacies. In the bustling hub of Miami, Richard Clément continues to infuse his creative energy into this project, enriching the narrative tapestry with his unique perspective and zest for life.

1

The Republicans

"In food we trust, I pledge allegiance to French cooking."

— Jean Pierre Labaguette US President

A cortège of government vehicles could be seen approaching from the edge of the High Line; two Chevy Suburban HD SUVs came to a screeching halt just outside the restaurant, and they parked right in front of it. One of the structures stood horizontally, while the other boasted a grilled facade that faced the esteemed establishment known as Chez Jean Pierre Labaguette.

Two men in black suits, white shirts, and red neckties

hopped out of the vehicles and initiated a safety protocol of the street. These men were body guards. they worked for the Republican Party. The agent's hands were positioned towards their waists, where both men packed heat in the form of Glock 17 automatic Luger pistol. They looked through their Aviator eyewear with dark green lenses and moved around frantically, inspecting their way and applying safety assessment tactics.

Once they were done, one of the men in the black suits spoke into his wrist. "This is Babysitter One; dry-cleaning is complete; the area is clean. Over," he raised one arm and moved his hand, making a circle.

Agent Number Two, now inside the restaurant, screened the interior for hidden cameras and microphones, repeating the line over his communication device: "All clear; GOP motorcade, proceed to destination. Over."

Three black limousines appeared from the corner of Washington Street and stopped near the SUVs. A dozen Republicans dressed formally in suits and neckties exited the three jalopies alongside four more guards in black suits and red ties.

In the vibrant Meatpacking District of New York City was the establishment owned by our future US president, renowned for its dedication to exquisite French cuisine. Positioned within the boundaries of Horatio Street to the South, West 16th Street to the north, the West Side Highway to the west, and Eighth Ave./Hudson Street to the east, this culinary gem captured the essence of its surroundings.

Following the tradition of the building architecture at the Meatpacking District, the Frenchman's restaurant was a part of the relatively new glass-and-steel developments that sprang up along the High Line, nevertheless retaining some of its old architectural characters thanks to the landmark guidelines.

Jean Pierre's restaurant sat on the bustling Washington Street, bustling with tourists and locals alike. Exquisite craftsmanship and meticulous attention to detail were invested in the restaurant's construction, resulting in a harmonious blend of elegant lines, premium materials, and refined aesthetics. The interior design embraced a modernist traveling theme, drawing inspiration from iconic French landmarks. Light colors, thoughtfully selected textures, and captivating forms adorned the space, creating an inviting ambiance that transported patrons on a visual journey reminiscent of France's cultural treasures.

Jean Pierre was recognized for his Northern European features: black hair, brown eyes, a large aquiline nose, and a beard. Adorned in the quintessential chef's attire, he sported a stylish beret atop his head. His classic white striped twill jacket featured sleek black Chinese collars and cuffs. Complementing his upper ensemble were well-tailored trousers and polished black Clark shoes, completing his distinguished appearance.

Emerging from their sleek limousines, the legion of Republicans meticulously fastened their suit buttons. Engaged in hushed conversations, their attention soon fixated on a single focal point—Jean Pierre Labaguette's restaurant. With determined strides and their collective gaze unwavering, they advanced towards the entrance.

One of the Republican Party executives said to his right-hand man, "This is the best French restaurant in New York; you are going love it."

"Yes, we need good food as much as we lack a good follow-up. We are going down to the polls; the next elections will be catastrophic if we do not get more voters."

"Welcome, gentlemen," Jean Pierre flashed his guests a huge burly, ear-to-ear smile.

"Hello, Jean Pierre," said one of the Republicans. One after the other, the suited men greeted him quickly, and it continued until they all exchanged pleasantries with him and his beautiful wife, Sylvie. Sylvie was a tall, slender Creole woman with dark hair and slight features. She was dressed in a white double-breasted jacket, pants in a black-and-white hound's-tooth pattern, and an apron hung from her neck, fastened to her slender waist.

Sylvie tilted her pretty head and whispered to her husband, "The Republican party team! Well, done, Jean Pierre." She spoke through a radiant, genial smile, "J'espère que vous allez les surcharger." [1]

Jean Pierre could only look at her with love in his eyes.

Jean Pierre did not move his eyes from his guests as he said in a low voice, "ils sont mes amis."[2] The smile was as if stuck to his slender face.

The Republican entourage was directed to one room, navigating through tables packed tightly with furniture, pushed against the walls, whose colors were chosen to feel very much 'on show.' The volumes of furniture, accessories, and light sources were far more significant, so there was a distraction from the color. The place was filled with hungry people with super-busy movements of the waiters who catered to the customers as

---

[1] I hope you will overcharge them.
[2] "They are my friends, and yes, I will overcharge them, mon amour."

they whizzed by the tables.

The scent of fresh food cooking hit the new arrivals and aroused their appetites—pictures of French cities from Nice to Bordeaux. Hung on the walls, the light fittings were set up to give a warm, snug-as-a-bug-in-rug ambiance.

The tables were occupied by patrons already there before the cavalry arrived. A hum of whispers and murmurs filled the restaurant, and the two security men shifted their glances from one table to another, from one group of customers to another. They all looked back at the pair wearing shades indoors and speaking into their wrists.

As the two men entered quietly into the restaurant, the tables were spread out so much that each felt secluded and, in contrast to the friendliness and liveliness of tables set very close to each other. Jean Pierre led them to a room where the guest's experience would be intimate.

The Republicans entered a room that served as a division between the bar and restaurant area. It was dark, with sumptuous, carefully selected restaurant chairs, tables, and accent pieces featuring bespoke items of furniture that resonated with the chef's ethos and, in turn, the restaurant's atmosphere. This style was exclusive to this one room, divided into two sections, with deep, Chesterfield-inspired banquettes in cherry red leather. Such furniture choices reinforced the menu's classic French cuisine message, combining comfort with unwavering quality. All the Republicans sat under a wooden ceiling draped with crystal chandelier, while in another, herringbone tile floors and textured, graphic wall panels glowed under a convex skylight.

"Gentlemen," Jean Pierre addressed the Republicans,

"Sommes-nous tous bien assis?"[3]

"What?" One of the Republicans frowned as he looked up at Jean Pierre.

"I apologize. Are we all pleasantly seated? And would you like to order any drinks, messieurs?" Which they did, and the drinks were served within minutes.

Standing next to her husband, Sylvie explained to the legislative assembly what the day's specialties were and assured them of taking as much time as they'd like to decide on their food orders. She went on to describe the menu to them.

"Bonsoir messieurs," the smile never left her glowing, desirable face and sexy lips. "Today, we have the following served for lunch," she handed a couple of menu cards over to the Republicans. "We also have some new dishes that are better than a vacation in Paris," this made everyone laugh.

"Really?" Asked one of the Republicans, with an oval face and prescription glasses. He was a heavy-set man in his late thirties, with piercing eyes and a receding hairline. "Is that true, Sylvie?"

Another group member glanced up from the menu, casting a brief look at Sylvie before turning their attention to Jean Pierre. "Please, enlighten us about your selections," they urged.

"There's Boeuf Bourguignon, a classic French beef stew made with red wine, pearl onions, mushrooms, and bacon. Once you try it, this dish will become a regular on your menu!" He paused for a beat, "We also have Coq au Vin, a simplified version of the classic red wine chicken stew from Burgundy."

---

[3] "Are we all sitting comfortably?"

"Sounds delicious," one of the Republicans said out loud.

"Wait, there's more, Monsieur... Potatoes Dauphinoise," JP added. "Out of all the ways to cook potato, this is one of the best."

The caucus seemed impressed as they nodded their heads in approval.

Jean Pierre continued, "Cassoulet, Lamb Chops, you will want to lick the Cognac Dijon Cream Sauce out of your plate! Très Magnifique."

"Chicken Cordon Bleu; Quiche Lorraine with hash brown crust. For those who would like something light, we have bouchée a la Reine; it is the world's finest starter, with Velvety béchamel sauce oozing out everywhere."

The Republicans' stomachs emitted low growls, a telltale sign of hunger echoing through the room.

Sylvie and Jean Pierre waited at their table for some more. "Chérie," she looked to her husband, "You're forgetting the Jambon-Beurre sandwich sample."

She turned to the guests and continued, "A good baguette topped with European butter and great quality ham. It will be love at first bite, I guarantee!"

"I suppose we should bring in the starters while you decide," Jean Pierre said.

"What will you get us?"

"Please let one of our waiters, who is dedicated to waiting at your table, know your preference for drinks."

"Mon Petit Four," a Republican tried to speak in French

but fell out of context.

"Excuse me?" Sylvie and Jean Pierre both spoke at once.

"Nothing, nothing, please go on..." the heavy-set, bespectacled Republican waved his hand in dismissal.

"Lyonnaise Salad, made of frisée lettuce, tossed in a warm and delicious vinaigrette and topped with crispy bacon and a poached egg. Concombre a La Menthe is made of sliced cucumbers and mint with a fuss-free yogurt dressing. French lentils with Dijon Vinaigrette; Gougerers; Palmiers..." he paused for a second, "anything you want, messieurs."

The Republicans decide what to order as Jean Pierre and Sylvie disappear toward the kitchen. The waiter was on standby with a notepad and pen. He made sure he appeared pleasant, welcoming, helpful, and neat. He smiled as he made eye contact and gave them his name, Walter. "Would you like to get us water, Walter?"

"Yes, please," said a few, "No, we'll go straight for the drinks," declared the rest.

The party of guests gracefully conveyed their drink preferences to Walter, who nodded with a genial smile before departing the enclosure. He returned in less than a minute, accompanied by the busser— a vision of elegance in her pristine white jacket and impeccably tailored black pants. Her presence added an aura of charm to the moment, enhancing the ambiance of the gathering.

"Good afternoon," she flashed a smile, and some men looked at her in a particular way, like the fox dressed as the granny in Goldilocks. Some even whispered to the ones sitting next to them about the new entrant.

"I'm Veronica. I'll be serving you the drinks."

"How lovely."

"You're so hot, Veronica."

"I think I lost my appetite to your full breasts and that round butt."

"Excuse me?" Veronica overheard 'round butt' and ignored it; the young lady was always struggling between her job at the restaurant and the unwarranted dalliance of the abusive elderly guests. These were high-profile guests. And she needed the job.

"Here you go," Veronica smiled despite her cringe.

Drinks and appetizers were served, followed by the first-course dish.

"Here you are, gents."

Walter and other waiters served the drinks. They lifted them off the tray and handled the glasses of Martini, Old Fashioned, Moscow Mule, Dark and stormy, Bellini, Gin and Tonic, Sidecar, Margarita, Vieux Carré, and White Russian with bottles of Evian Water by handling the glasses from the bottom. The universal rule of serving glassware by their stem handles or the bottom of the glass and general rules of etiquette were in full effect here. Jean Pierre had trained his staff well.

Suddenly, a hush fell over the table, and the clinking of tableware hitting plates became the only audible sound. Moments later, the main course arrived, eliciting murmurs of anticipation. As the first bite was savored, it became evident that the food was nothing short of exquisite, delighting the senses with each mouthful.

Jean Pierre entered the room and asked, "Are we all doing

good, gentlemen?"

"Yes, Jean Pierre, very well, the food is delicious," said the Republican with the receding hairline.

"Thank you, monsieur. Would the good people like dessert?" They looked at each other.

"You won't regret it; I promise," the smile never once left JP's face.

"Oh, what the heck, what have you got, Jean Pierre?"

2

The Future President Restaurant

"Cooking and politics are more than just about ingredients and mixing".

— **Jean Pierre Labaguette US President**

Jerry Bilac, a prominent figure within the Republican-leaning independent camp, distinguished himself not only by his weight but also by his oval face and scholarly glasses. While many in his group identified as 'socially conservative,' Senator Bilac traversed further into neo-conservatism, aligning himself with the anti-establishment wing. His political journey commenced in the late 2000s, marked by a profound sense of insight and an astute comprehension of the intricate political terrain. With steadfast determination and unwavering dedication, he navigated the complexities of the political landscape, steadily ascending to his esteemed position within the U.S. government.

"Relatively speaking. Each country has free-market aspects," he sipped his drink and continued, "although there is no such thing as a pure free market, it's more a concept than a tangible reality," he enlightened the man sitting next to him, Ted Dumby, who was also a neoconservative.

"The Grand Party (GOP)..." he cast his words like ingots, his mouth a metal refinery while chewing and swallowing a bite of Chicken Cordon Bleu. "...Has decided to support lower taxes, deregulation, increased military spending, gun rights, restrictions on abortion," he paused to wipe his mouth with a table napkin and said, "Damn, this was delicious, I must bring Lorain here."

He billeted off his wife as he washed down the flavor, the sophistication of a healthier baked version of the dish with a sip of White Russian.

"Haven't you had too much to drink?" asked Bilac.

Dumby shook his head and waved a hand, saying, "No restrictions on immigration and restrictions on labor unions. We are the ones who were strongly committed to protectionism and tariffs at its founding, but I see a pattern here: Bilac is more supportive of free trade. Because there are federal minimum wages and antitrust laws; regulations imposed by government agencies like the SEC; and corporate taxes, along with import and export tariffs."

"That doesn't make sense, Senator," Bilac winced. "How do you do that?"

"Do what?" Ted Dumby scrutinized Bilac.

"Never mind, you were saying."

Jean Pierre interrupted and asked them if they were ready for dessert. They certainly were.

"Take, for instance, the conservative think tank Heritage Foundation's 2021 Index of Economic Freedom, which ranks nations on a 100-point scale, gives the U.S. a score of 75, which places it in the second tier 'mostly free' category."

"Yes, and what about it?" Senator Bilac queried.

"The U.S. fares a little better in the 'Economic Freedom of the World: 2020 Annual Report,' issued by the Fraser Institute of Canada, another think tank. It comes in sixth or seven places on the world rankings roster—squarely in the highest 'most free' category."

"Most free? Really?"

"Yes, and yes."

"So, what you're trying to say is..."

"Hong Kong ranks as number one on the list overall."

"No, no..." Bilac shook his head as a roar of laughter arose from another table filled with Republicans. He brought his attention back to the matter at hand, "On the other end of the spectrum, there are countries that are considered 'repressed,' as that good-for-nothing Heritage Foundation puts it. These countries have virtually no economic freedoms."

"... If the government removed this law, people are free to

wear or not wear the seatbelt without the threat of being reprimanded. This also extends into the business world. For instance, removing the minimum wage would be an example of deregulation..." Three Republicans at the far end of the tables were talking amongst themselves.

"...Black and Hispanic workers get a larger boost from unionization. Black workers represented by a union are paid 13.7% more than their nonunionized peers. Hispanic workers represented by unions are paid 20.1% more than their nonunionized peers..." Another group was speaking on the matter of restrictions on the labor union.

Dumby was a man in his forties and was less popular within his peer group than he would have liked. However, the top echelon 'liked him' because of his radicalized views that sometimes worked like a charm for the country and those running it into the ground.

Dumby was a tall man with a lean frame; the stitching and the fit of his Saville Row suit were as sharp as the steak knife; he held in his right hand. He wore glasses that he kept perching up by wrinkling his nose. "Which, er..." he paused momentarily and turned to look toward the bar where Jean Pierre had disappeared.

"Hey, Walter."

"Yes, Senator?"

"I'm not a Senator, well, not yet."

"I'm sorry, Senat... Mr.," Walter panicked.

Before the entourage arrived at Jean Pierre's restaurant, J.P. had meticulously briefed all his employees on the names and designations of the lunch guests they would be hosting or serving. With an air of professionalism and keen attention to detail, Veronica and her fellow bussers were also entrusted with a similar task for patrons awaiting tables reserved for Republican guests.

"Ted Dumby."

Walter looked at him with confusion and asked, "I'm sorry, did you say Ted Bundy?"

"I get that all the time, that idiot. It would've been Fred Dumby had my father not deliberately misspelled my name on the birth certificate. I come from a matriarchal family; men don't or can't do much."

Walter nodded with his hands folded before him. "Yes, sir?"

"Yeah, please see if you can find Jean Pierre for us."

"Certainly, Mr. Bu... Dumby," Walter said as he almost ran out of the annex. His French whitish face was dark brownish and bordered on red.

"So, yeah, I was saying," Senator Bilac continued, but another group of Republicans laughed out loud. 'What the fuck?" He said, frowning, "I'm not taking this rowdy drunk-ass bunch back to the office like this."

"Aww, c'mon, they're just having a good time."

"On a weekday, in the middle of the afternoon?"

Dumby did not say anything but listened to what the commotion was about. "The president's trip abroad does at least provide some respite from the relentless social media-led madness of his time in office. And this is the perfect time for us to position our puppet."

He heard someone say, followed by, "Maybe he will form his political party. Perhaps he'll start his very own television network. There's also the distinct possibility he will get a visit from the police before too long."

Sylvie stood at the entrance to the private enclosure. Standing below a soft, warm light shade, a halo formed around her face. Bilac removed his glasses and wiped them with the table napkin. He said, "You look like an Angel."

"Peut-être parce qu'elle est un angel,"[4] said J.P.

Sylvie took hold of his hand lovingly. "Hope you guys enjoyed your meal?" Everyone agreed in unison, as a few applauded.

"What next, a standing ovation for Walter?" Dumby thought.

Sylvie said something to the waiters behind her, "s'il vous plaît servez."[5]

Once again, the entire table went quiet as dessert was served, except for one of the politicians, Steven, who had too many shots of Bellini with his Lamb Chops cooked in Cognac Dijon Cream Sauce.

"A man goes to Heaven and meets Jesus."

"Go on," the others said.

"Well, Jesus is showing him around," he said as he spotted a broken clock.

"What's that there for?" he asked.

---

[4] "Maybe because she's an angel."
[5] "Please serve."

"Jesus says, that's Mother Teresa's clock; it has never moved because she has never lied."

"Get over with it already, Rourke."

"Just over here is Abraham Lincoln's clock. He lied twice, so it has moved twice."

Nobody laughed. This time, Bilac spoke, "Hey Rourke, you done?"

"No, no. Wait for the punchline."

"I hate to break it to you, but this isn't some off-site chill-out activity."

Rourke has yet to respond.

"Oh, well, OK. What's the god dammed punchline."

"Where is the president's clock?" asked the man.

"Jesus answers, 'It's in my office; I'm using it as a ceiling fan."

There was silence before the enclosure erupted in a mirthful chant. They couldn't stop laughing. Jean Pierre still stood at the entrance to the private enclosure. He interjected with a polite "Ahm."

Bilac and Dumby looked over their Profiteroles and Crème brûlée. "Oh, hey, Jean Pierre."

"At your service, our future leaders."

"Check, please. These guys can't seem to follow protocol."

He nodded and vanished once again with Walter. Leaving Veronica waiting for the drunks and a less-than-sober table.

****

Back At the Republican Head Quarters

The entourage reached 315 State Street Albany, Buffalo, once a bastion of GOP Moderates, who carved out a niche by embracing the social.

Dumby and Bilac entered a room as the entourage dispersed, lit the lights, and drew the shades.

Senator Bilac was the first to speak, "Do you know about Francisco Franco? I mean, know about him?"

"I've heard of him, but please, go ahead, enlighten me."

"When a leftist coalition won Spanish elections in February 1936, General Francisco Franco was packed off to a remote post in the Canary Islands. Though privy to a coup plot brewing among his fellow army officers, he initially hesitated to join, finally becoming convinced following the retaliatory assassination of a conservative politician.

I kept mixing up on July 18 or the 20th, and Franco broadcast a manifesto imploring the military to overthrow the democratically elected government. As army garrisons across Spain heeded his call, he secretly flew from the Canary Islands to Spanish-controlled Morocco, where the uprising began a day earlier. He took charge of the battle-hardened troops stationed there."

"Huh, you say that as if Francesco was taking a walk in the park," Dumby confirmed as he took out his Glock, unloaded it, and sheathed it.

"Dumby, I mean Franco, was able to ferry them across to the Spanish mainland with the help of Fascist Italy and Nazi

Germany. The coup attempt was only partially successful, leaving Franco's rebels in control of just one-third of the country and precipitating a bloody civil war that would last three years. In the end, though, he emerged victorious. With the support of fascists, monarchists, the landed gentry, and the Catholic Church, 'El Caudillo' would rule as dictator of Spain until he died in 1975."

"Ummm hmmm... And?"

"And nothing."

"What's going through your head?" asked Dumbly, concerned.

The Senator revealed, "If we had a political chief as good in rhetoric as the culinary speech of Jean Pierre, we would win the elections."

"What?" Dumby's face contorted. He was dumbfounded. "Jean Pierre? He's not even a true American. You're kidding, right? Please say you do not want a French president. And are you sure he's Catholic? I'm pretty sure he holds other beliefs except for the traditions and beliefs of Catholic Churches."

"Oh, that can be sorted, like it was with Obama," Bilac unstrapped his belt and hung it to the coat stand; the gun's weight made the belt swing for a while.

"Obama was Catholic. Remember 2008; Obama stepped up his effort to correct the misconception that he was Muslim when the presidential campaign had hit the Bible? John F. Kennedy and Joe Biden are our only Catholic presidents," he paused to breathe.

"Did you have a conversation with him, I mean, besides what the entire group and Jean Pierre exchanged?"

Bilac did not answer; he slumped into one of the office chairs with a thump.

"If we can do something about the NRA, we will win the elections – you know there have been twenty-seven school and civilian shootings since the year started, and it's only fucking June, for Christ's sake?"

"That's karma. What goes around comes around in the form of disturbed teenage lone gunmen with a thing for their grandmothers and first-person shooters."

"Huh?"

"Drones, that too, unmanned cowards. Forget it. We will need a speech coach for him to get rid of the European accent."

"He doesn't have a European accent."

"Yes, he does."

****

3

Looking for a Candidate

"L'habit ne fait pas le moine"

"Clothes don't make the man."

The blue sky above Buffalo, NY, suddenly started to change color. It went from being deeply cerulean to a formation of cotton pewter. Then, after a while, the downpour started. The raindrops struck the office building of the Republicans and drummed wildly on the glass windows, making them quiver slightly, as a crack of lightning lit the sky in a bright flash of pristine white.

Followed by a loud booming sound, moving heavily, after which rumbles and cracks accompanied the lightning during the thunderstorm. Furious rain and hail relentlessly pounded the building's exterior, triggering a wave of nostalgia among war veterans who had transitioned into influential political figures and top executives of oil companies. The tempestuous weather reminded them of their days in Vietnam, particularly in the dense jungles of Da Nang in South Vietnam. Fond memories resurface of the relentless rain that saturated the landscapes during those days when the North Vietnamese Army persistently sought to breach the defenses of the South.

When the downpour ceased, the mosquitoes seemed to take on the role of the adversary. Following them, the challenges shifted to navigating through swamps, climbing hills, dealing with leeches, and seeking refuge in bunkers amidst the heat. Even amidst the discomfort, there's a sense of camaraderie and resilience that defined those moments, like pulling smoldering hot shrapnel out of a fellow soldier.

Senator Bilac and his one-down, Dumby, a pluviophile, and the rest at the headquarters jumped a little from their seats whenever lightning flashed across the sky, followed by the brash thunk.

"That is one heavy downpour," one of the Republicans exclaimed.

"No shit, Michio Kaku," another member of the Old Guard snapped back at him.

"Cut it out, guys," Senator Bilac raised his voice, and the room went silent. The hailstorm and the cascading continued, with an even louder outrage, making the Republicans' shackles rise.

Bilac thought, looking at the ominous environment, "There is a new war on the way. A political war is on the horizon."

When the conversation resumed, other than opposing Joe Biden, the tête-à-tête between the men shifted to the age-old adage of tax reforms.

"There is universal opposition to Democrats' proposals to boost taxes on upper-income Americans," Jerry Quagmire said with disdain. "Levy tax on the homeless and leave the mansions on Long Island alone, for they will get upset otherwise, which means the vote bank is going bust. The fucking Dems want their own, the less than half per cent of almost 300 million residents, or people or donkeys or workers on an urban plantation, McDonald's, Wendy's, White Castle."

He paused, "Nearly half of all Americans are employed by small businesses."

"The 'working poor' spend twenty-seven weeks or more in a year in the labor force either working or looking for work, but whose incomes fall below the poverty level, you're right, Jerry," Col Harry Angel spoke with an unlit cigarette in his mouth. "According to the US Bureau of Labor Statistics, 2020, about 9.5 million people who spent at least 4536 hours in the labor force were from poor families." Col. Angel was a tall, well-built man in his late Sixties. He was a heavy smoker and kept an unlit ciggy in his mouth whenever indoors.

"We need more voters," Jefferson Groundplain spoke. "Black vote matters, Asian vote matters, Latin vote matters..." His gaze swept across the room, observing a mix of individuals. Some directed their attention towards the rain and hail, peering out the window, while others turned to engage in conversation. It became apparent to everyone present that the room lacked diversity, as there were no Asians, blacks, or women in the vicinity.

Instead, the occupants were white Caucasian men, comfortably seated in task chairs with mesh backrests. With feet casually resting on the table and hands casually folded behind their heads, they exuded an air of relaxed confidence. "We have that racist wasp image."

"... Conservative on social issues, pro-life, anti-gun control, the self-styled party of family values," Senator Bilac pitched in, but no one except Dumby heard him.

Suddenly, as the thunderstorm showed signs of calming down, they all started speaking simultaneously.

"Who is going to be our party candidate?"

"We have Ronald, Jeff, and Glenn so far."

"This is a nightmare."

"They all have dark secrets; if they get elected, we will get a backlash. We need somebody clean, new, fresh."

****

The following day, a Wednesday, Senator Jerry Bilac and Ted Dumby were back at the Jean Pierre Labaguette Restaurant. The two politicians were once again escorted by an entourage of security men in black suits and secret-agent shades by Tom Ford Gucci and Ray-Ban. They talked into their wrists and swept the area for any potential threats before the two Republicans could go about their lives.

Jerry and Ted stepped out of the chauffeur-driven, unmarked jalopy, a conspicuous emblem of wealth, distinction, and societal hierarchy that has long been both a physical and symbolic divider among people since the turn of the 20th century. As the doors closed behind them with a gentle thud and a faint popping sound, they were enveloped in an aura of privilege and exclusivity, marking their entrance into a world where such distinctions held sway.

"The land yacht is getting old," Dumby said. He bent a little as if he knew where the noise was coming from, and security parlance started to look at him with questioning eyes.

"Just what the heck are you doing?" Bilac asked Dumby.

Dumby replied, "The sound emanates from the lower hinge roller axle."

He then called out to Jackson. Secret Agent Jackson came running over like a dog with his weapon unsheathed.

"What, what happened? Where is he? Did you get a good look? Is there a window?" He frantically looked up and sideways; behind him, he ran to the curb and sprinted back until Dumby told him to calm down.

"I was only telling you that this flivver can use some grease between the roller pin and the inside surface."

"Oh, I thought..."

"Doesn't matter what you thought," he snapped back. "I'm pretty sure there's insufficient lube on the lower hinge roller axle. The greasing should correct this concern."

"Yes, sir, I'll notify the concerned department."

"What do you mean?"

The Secret Agent man, Jackson, looked confused as he said, "Huh? I mean, I'll ask the guys..."

"Just do it yourself when you're off duty. This is hardly the Charlie Hebdo shooting trial – nor the Watergate scandal, which reminds me. Hey Bilac, remind me to tell you something about Nixon."

"T'es vraiment emmerdant, toi Sacrebleu. Yes, Sir Mr. Dumby," Jackson agreed as he once again resumed position.

"Comme bonjour Messieurs! Good to see you again so soon. Please come in." Jean Pierre was alone. His wife Sylvie was inside the restaurant with Veronica and Walter.

The pair heard him and greeted him with a smile, and the three entered the restaurant. Their steps matched each other as they marched through the gate.

"Jean Pierre?" Bilac looked behind at him.

"Oui, mon bon monsieur?"

"Would you have time to talk?" whispered Dumby

"Ce sera mon Plaisir, c'est toujours avec gaitée que nous vous recevons."

"What does gaitée mean?" then suddenly angry he raised his voice. "First, you tell me, are you calling me gay?"

"Non," Jean Pierre's eyes become wide and apologetic. He spoke in French, "chacun voit midi à sa porte." He stopped. Then, after a long inhale, he responded, "I'm sorry, it means Pleasure."

"And the rest?"

Before he could answer, Veronica walked toward the bar in

the foreground. Dumby elbowed Bilac, who looked at Dumby and slightly shook his head.

"Good day, gentlemen," Sylvie greeted. "How nice it is to lay eyes on you people today again." The smile was still plastered from the first time they had dined here.

"Hello, Sylvia," Bilac greeted her. "We enjoyed your selection the other day. The food was excellent."

"Merci, Senator. It's Sylvie," she corrected him.

"Hi, Sylvie," Dumby greeted her.

"Today we have a whole range of Chicken Tarragon in aromatics crust – a specialty of Provence; Black Angus ribeye old fashioned mustard juice from the region of Lyon; Sea bass purple artichokes smoky and crispy from the French Rivi..."

"Unfortunately, we're not here for the food today, Sylvie."

"Yes, yes. Can we borrow your husband for a while?"

"Bien sûr... You can keep him; I'm tired of Jean Pierre," She laughed. The men eyed each other, and then Veronica caught their attention again.

"Man, I'd like to get soupe au poulet with her. I mean, look at the cleavage on her," Dumby thought, ogling the clothes off Sylvie when Jean Pierre noticed.

"Pisser dans un violon, she is taken, Senator Dumby."

"I'm not a senator, Jean Pierre, well, not yet. This guy here? You see him?"

They looked at Bilac, who was looking at Veronica's round, perfect butt, in those body-hugging black pants and an 'S' size shirt, with the top button undone and a tight white jacket, the uniform of a busser, slightly different from the other waiters. She bent to pick something off the floor, and the waistband of her white panty peeked out.

Dumby craned his neck and straightened up immediately. "This guy here is a senator. Not me, I'm NOT a senator, capish?"

"Yes, toutes mes excuses, I'm..."

"English, Jean Pierre, English. You're not in Paris anymore."

"Oui... I mean, of course, I'm sorry."

They then asked Jean Pierre to take them to a private room, far from the madding crowd of the occupied tables. They went into the secluded section of the restaurant, where the atmosphere was more cordial.

Dumby played with Philippe Patek on his wrist and got up, saying, "For heaven's sake, Jean Pierre, turn some lights on. It's darker than the future of Democracy in here."

Bilac gave a chuckle and extended his hand to Dumby, who held it and hoisted himself up. "My God."

Walter and a few other restaurant employees were everywhere they looked; hand sanitizers were mounted on one of the walls, polite yet detached workers were laying out fresh napkins, and the table runners on the dining tables were being changed. Even the chairs were being thoroughly wiped down.

"This should've been done before we came in," Bilac thought, touching the tactile way to where Jean Pierre was picking up wine glasses and inspecting those.

****

"Can I get you drinks, gentlemen?" Walter asked.

"I'll have some sparkling water."

"And you, dear sir?' Walter looked at Dumby, who looked at Bilac. He turned his head back to Walter and saw Veronica walk in.

"Hey, Veronica." Dumby flashed the biggest smile ever.

Veronica waved back and darted out as quickly as she had entered. Ah, screw it... "Wait, wait... er..."

"Walter." He reminded Dumby.

"Yes, get me Stoli on the rocks."

"One sparkling water for you and Stoli on ice for the other gent. I'll be right back with your drinks, gentlemen." He zoomed a smile and hightailed out of the exclusive hole.

Bilac and Jean Pierre had already started a conversation, and Dumby said, "Listen carefully, Jean Pierre."

"Very carefully," Dumby added.

"I'm listening. Please go ahead."

Bilac continued, "We need minority votes to win the next elections, and we are looking for new fresh faces for the party, and we have someone perfect in mind."

"Yeah, you look like a perfect party member," Dumby interrupted. "The way you talk, your mannerisms, the way you carry yourself, and..."

"May I finish?" Bilac sounded flustered.

Dumby looked at him, then looked away towards the entrance as he watched Walter enter with their drinks.

"Here you go, gents." He gently placed the water bottle and Dumby's drink on the table and walked away, picking up his stride.

"A peaceful transfer of power, particularly from one political party to another." Bilac took a deep breath before continuing. "That's what we have in mind, the ultimate expression of the rule of law and a society governed by the law, not by individual rulers."

Not realizing the contradiction in his rhetoric, Bilac kept his eyes locked with Jean Pierre, who couldn't seem to stop nodding, like an Indian corporate executive whose head keeps shaking like a dashboard ornament, a JP bobblehead.

"Say what you want about him, but it was George Washington's great contribution to the American political tradition when he voluntarily gave up the presidency. It established an unbroken tradition of presidents yielding power, including to their bitter political opponents." He keenly looked at Jean Pierre, who expressed tractable boredom.

"Are you gents sure you don't want to order today's special? Oysters. We have blue cheese such as Bleu D'Auvergne or goat cheese. Then monkfish with Chorizo, soft-ripened cheese such as brie or camembert, or a firmer cheese such as Morbier?"

Bilac put two fingers on the front of his forehead and rubbed the skin there, saying, "We're not here for food today, Jean Pierre." Bilac frowned and shut his eyes, tired of repeating himself. "I think we told Sylvia

"Sylvie."

"Jesus, yes, yes, my goodness. Sylvie."

"Sylvie," Jean Pierre repeated, unable to understand why

Bilac had difficulty correctly taking his wife's name.

Bilac cleared his throat and continued, "Even on the cusp of the Civil War, for example, James Buchanan never suggested that Abraham Lincoln wasn't entitled to become president after he won the election. That's what's so unprecedented with the current transition process; there is no legal path for our actual president to remain president. The spectacle of an incumbent president behaving this way, with school shootings occurring almost weekly, with the dollar falling..."

Jean Pierre cleared his throat.

Bilac ignored him and continued, "And that is something we haven't seen before and is deeply corrosive to our Democracy. Now, here's the point."

He leaned in and whispered, "Would you like to join our party?

Jean Pierre became all bright-eyed and bushy tailed. Looking at Dumby, he asked, "You're joking, right?"

"Not one bit," Bilac said. "Blacks are too extreme, Asians cannot be trusted, Hispanics are too many, French is enough ethnic and fresh."

Jean Pierre said, "Cooking and food is like politics. You need the guests, the audience, to crave for the food – before they taste it – like a political program, dream about the savors, and smell the flavors."

"Yes, exactly."

"I wish our political achievements will be as good as we promise. It is rarely the case, I must admit." Bilac continued, "Jean Pierre, do you want to join our dream team?"

"Sorry, my friends, I am not in politics," He smiled. "My dream is to bring good food and good eating habits to America."

"Maybe we could make you more famous and help you rack up your dream," Bilac said, emphasizing 'more famous.' He went on, "We could help you open other restaurants in Washington, Los Angeles, Miami, Truth or Consequences, wherever you want. You will change the taste buds of America."

"Alright. Are you sure you're not hungry?"

"Not for food," Dumby laughed.

"Ok, maybe something sweet, a cherry clafoutis, a creamy dessert served with black cherries, baked in a pancake-like batter. A portion of the simple batter of eggs, sugar, milk, flour, and vanilla is first baked to create a stable base, then the cherries and remaining batter are added before baking again until set. A dusting of powdered sugar is the finishing to..."

"Goddammit, we don't want any dessert either, JP!" Bilac was evidently running out of patience. He got up and looked at Dumby, who was looking at the door to this room in hopes of Veronica walking in."

Bilac snapped his fingers thrice. Snap! Snap! Snap!

"What is the matter with you?" Dumby asked. "Do you want me to dance? Why are you snapping like that?

"Dumby, stop drinking and get yourself together."

"Yessir, Mr. Senator." He raised the right hand sharply, fingers and thumb extended and joined, palm facing down, as he placed the tip of the right forefinger on his temple, slightly to the right of the eye.

Bilac rolled his eyes. "Jean Pierre."

"Yes?"

Bilac took out his business card, held JP's hand, turned it, palm up, and slammed the card on it, like in a game of Split. "Call me. I need you to see our Albany, Buffalo office ASAP."

"What's ASAP?"

"Where's Veronica? Bring her along?" Dumby interrupted.

Jean Pierre looked at Dumby's wedding ring and shook his head.

Bilac told his bodyguard, "Terry, take Mr. Dumby back to the car. I don't suppose he can walk on his own."

"I can bloody well sprint 100 meters, and Terry and Jackson will never catch me." He got up and bumped into a couch, "God..."

He saw Veronica as she entered and said, "Jean Pierre, Sylvie would like to see you."

"Tell her I'll be with her shortly."

"Er, now? She says it's urgent."

Jean Pierre looked at Bilac.

"Go to your wife, Jean Pierre, but remember, you have to be at the given address within three days or less." He looked towards Dumby, who was once again staring at Veronica with his big, round eyes.

"Veronica, you're perfect." Dumby spurted out.

"Thank you, Mr. Bundy."

"Ted, Ted Bundy, the charismatic, almost-lawyer serial killer, who broke out of jail twice." He laughed as Veronica left the room.

"Where'd she goes? Did I say something?"

Jean Pierre changed the topic, "I'll be there, Senator Bilac, don't worry, but I have to go now; Sylvie is waiting."

"I will be your father figure. Put your tiny hand in mine, I..." Dumby hiccupped. "Will be your preacher-teacher, anything you want me to, I will be... I will be your daaaadeeeee..."

The security men approached Dumby from the back and lifted him, "Hey, hey..."

"To the car," Bilac said. "I'll see you soon, Jean Pierre."

He signaled a thumbs up and walked out.

****

The following week, after a talk with Sylvie, in which she had stated that she was adamant about opening more restaurants, Jean Pierre went to the Republican headquarters, and the staff briefed him.

In another room, Bilac and Ted discussed the future party.

Ted said, "We have three candidates: Ronald, Jeff, and Glenn."

"Glenn? But he's part Hispanic," whispered Dumby

"And Ronald looks Brazilian to me," Dumby added, sitting on the pleather couch again.

"Ronald has so many legal lawsuits, Ponzi, and scams that we cannot endorse him," Bilac sounded concerned and cornered.

"What about Jeff? He seems that he had some sex with an underage teenager, and she is black," Dumby made the lack of color blindness most conspicuous.

"No good, no good."

"And Glenn, his father was KKK; we are screwed. There isn't a good candidate."

A phone rang. Bilac answered, "Jerry Bilac here."

"A Jean Pierre is here; he says he wants to see you."

"Send him in, Maggie."

"Jean Pierre's here," Bilac informed Dumby.

****

Jean Pierre entered the room hunched, wearing a tweed jacket and slacks over brown loafers. "Hello, Senator. Hello, Mr. Dumby."

"Hey, JP, my man!" Dumby got off the chair to greet him.

"Did you say I can open restaurants nationwide if I do what you guys tell me?"

"Yes, I did. Are you a Republican, Jean Pierre?"

"I wake up Democrat, I go to sleep Republican, and I am a Liberal during my vacations," answered Jean Pierre with a smile.

"We will have all our political meals in your restaurants."

"All over the US?" Jean Pierre added.

"All over the United States of America, le français!"

"I will join your party."

"Our dream team."

"Oui oui. les premiers de cordées."

"Er, you mean let's do it."

"Same things…" JP said as he half smiled and looked away.

4

Business Deal

« Je cuisine – donc je suis »

— Jean Pierre Labaguette US President

Back at 315 State Street Albany, Buffalo, three men were seated in a private office that Senator Bilac had booked before they could invite Jean Pierre to the GOP headquarters a second time. Senator Jerry Bilac and Ted Dumby stepped out of the office when Jean Pierre and Sylvie arrived. They took the elevator two floors down to the reception, where Jean Pierre stood with an ear-to-ear smile. Margarette Cobblepot, the twenty-three-year-old receptionist with blue hair, kept stealing glances at the couple, who were dressed elegantly.

Jean Pierre had his beret on. He was wearing a plain white cotton shirt with a jewel blue bow tie knotted in a typical shoelace knob. Jean Pierre adorned himself with a unique ensemble, donning a pair of charcoal and mint suspenders that snugly embraced his waist, secured by a flexible elastic belt. These suspenders accompanied the classic plaid French grid trousers, while his feet found solace in shiny black, lace-up derby shoes sans socks. The culturally aware French cook also donned a regatta striped blazer—maroon and blue—with two buttons, a single-breasted design, notched lapels, and flap pockets. Jean Pierre radiated flamboyance, his attire perfectly complementing his striking good looks. He was a charismatic, talented visionary and dressed like one.

Sylvie exuded an irresistible sense of style, a trait she shared with her husband. With effortless grace, she flaunted her fashion-forward selections, donning a Black Wool and Cashmere Knit Cardigan adorned with the Dior pixel zodiac motif. Her ensemble continued to mesmerize, featuring a zipped dress in a striking blend of yellow and black, fashioned in the Check'n'Dior Wool Twill pattern. With every elegant movement, Sylvie transformed into a living, breathing embodiment of Dior's timeless allure, effortlessly captivating all who beheld her.

Sylvie said, "Tu dois aller rencontrer les républicains, mon amour."[6]

---

[6] "You have to go meet the Republicans, my love!"

"Je ne sais pas chérie, je pense qu'ils jouent avec moi,"[7] Jean Pierre replied.

"Ne sois pas' bête, tu as toujours été paranoïaque Jean Pierre."[8]

"Have I ?"

"Oui."

"OK si tu le dis."[9]

Margarette couldn't help herself after looking at the woman who looked a bit recherché for your average visitor at the Republican headquarters. Sylvie looked like a dazzling, colorful, ravishingly exquisite bumblebee. Miss Cobblepot stood on her toes and bent forward a little to see what the French lady had on as footwear. It was a pair of Dior Symbol Ankle Boots made of supple black calfskin. The twenty-three-year-old receptionist couldn't help but compliment both, especially Sylvie, on her attire, the boots, and the double-circled emblem on the side, 'Christian Dior Paris.'

"Hello, Miss...?"

"Mrs. Labaguette, Sylvie Labaguette," Sylvie answered as she looked at Margarette, who was decked in an austere manner. Sylvie glanced at the receptionist's formal, sober, stringent outfit; the upper part of her body visible from across the reception desk. Margarette wore a skirt or slacks. Sylvie couldn't tell as half of her was blocked by a clean, uncluttered white, slanted, custom-made office reception desk. It was crafted from a durable Corian Solid Surface. The desk boasted a solid wood

---

[7] "I don't know sweetheart; I think they're playing with me."
[8] "Don't be silly, you've always been paranoid, Jean Pierre."
[9] "Ok. If you say so..."

construction, exquisitely designed to create a welcoming atmosphere. Careful attention was paid to the furnishing's arrangement, ensuring visitors were not crowded together while maintaining a sense of closeness.

As Sylvie glanced around, her eyes landed on a professional attire that caught her attention. A plain white jacket blouse perfectly complemented a solid black single-breasted regular-fit blazer. The combination was of understated style and timeless sophistication.

"Mrs. Labaguette..."

"Call me Sylvie."

"Mrs. Sylvie..."

"Just Sylvie."

"Sylvie, I love your bag and boots. Christian Dior?"

Sylvie viewed her clothes and then raised her head, "Yes, isn't it obvious."

Margarette thought of saying, "Yes, it's screaming designer wear, especially with the black and white monogrammed badge to increase awareness, and the superstitious iconography of Christian Dior, complete with the stylized letters "C" and "D," making them mirror images of each." But instead, she said, "it is, Sylvie."

Margarette felt a little chided. She was only complimenting the lady, not asking her to let her borrow the lavish and expensive handbag or the sleek boots that the French lady wore.

"Jean Pierre! Sylvie!" Dumby had a blank-courteous smile on his round face. He extended his hand while still a few feet away from them, "How is it going, guys?"

"La vie est un beau rêve, mais ne nous réveillez pas,"[10] Jean Pierre shrugged as the couple shook hands with Dumby and then Bilac. Both Hawks wore black staple suits with navy patterned ties and gold cufflinks. Dumby was wearing a Baum & Mercier Riviera this time instead of the Philippe Patek on his wrist, and the senator had a classic, two-tone Rolex clasped around his left wrist like he always did.

"English Jean Pierre," Bilac paused as he looked at Margarette, who was looking down at some papers on her desk and then answered a call. "We don't want..."

Dumby jumped in, lowering his voice, and came close to Jean Pierre, "Yeah, man, we don't want them," he tilted his head towards Margarette and continued, the others to know."

"Know what?"

"That you're not American."

"But I am," His smile became crooked. "Life is a beautiful dream, but don't wake up."

"Excuse me?" Dumby frowned.

"Never mind," Bilac tried to find words or memories that reminded him of the fragrance. He dug deeper to find meaningful connections. "Does he smell soft notes of May rose and Italian iris? To Neroli from Grasse in southern France, this perfume has a wonderfully romantic scent. What could it be?" Bilac thought.

"That's some unique, refreshing perfume that you're wearing, Sylvie," he complimented but was interjected by

---

[10] "Life is a beautiful dream, but don't wake up."

Dumby.

Dumby assumed a highly formal demeanor and expressed, "Jean Pierre, if you are an American, we want you to be our presidential candidate."

"Can you prove it?"

"I can do that easily, but I do not want to be your presidential candidate. I am not a politician, just a great chef."

"Cherie," Sylvie came closer to JP.

"Oui chérie?"[11]

"Take it."

"Qu'est-ce que tu veux dire?[12] Say yes to the gentlemen for becoming a candidate for the president of the United States."

"Are you serious, my love?"

"Aussi sérieux que le plat principal.[13] I will be the first Lady we can make that country better."

Jean Pierre looked at Bilac and Dumby and said, "Will I be able to make positive changes."

"Carte Blanche, if you show us your birth certificate."

"Alright, Oui, d'accord."[14]

Dumby looked at the to-be power couple, and so did Margarette. "Delightfully delicate and powdery note of cedar wood, which is spicy and human but also reminiscent of pencil

---

[11] "Yes, dear?"
[12] "What do you mean?"
[13] "As serious as the main course."
[14] "Yes, OK."

shavings, with pepper and orchid for contrast? What is your perfume, Miss... I mean Sylvie?" The receptionist asked, utterly oblivious to the little conversation the couple just exchanged, flipping the future of America a birdie with their pinkies.

"Nina Ricci L'Air du Temps," Sylvie answered, with a straight face as she adjusted her short hair. "It is by Nina Ricci. Created in 1948 by Francis Fabron and Nina Ricci's son Robert, it is meant for married women rather than young girls...." Sylvie looked at Margarette, once again making her feel rebuked; she continued, "With notes of carnation, sandalwood, gardenia, and rose, its subtle floral tones are rather pleasing to the mature woman." She looked to her husband, who stood tall, exuding leadership and assertiveness, and was smiling.

"How lovely," Dumby jumped in.

"Shall we go to the office? We can talk all we want there."

"Thanks, my friend. We opened two restaurants with your funding. I am so proud – Un million de Merci," With the smile still cemented on his face, Jean Pierre crossed his legs as he updated the two Hawks.

"How nice," Bilac replied as he fiddled with a Faber Castell and rolled it between his fingers like a drummer in between a drum roll.

The office looked like IKEA threw up in it, except for a black Kathy Ireland computer armoire, which housed stacks of paper and office supplies, a bunch of folders and files, and a contract. Bilac and Jean Pierre sat around a brown-black corner desk with metal legs, swivel-mesh chairs, and a high-back leather chair. On the tables positioned along the opposite wall, a laser printer and an inkjet printer rested, ready for use. Adjacent to them, brown-black corner bookshelves proudly stood in the corner of the office. One of the shelves hosted a collection of fiction literature. At the same time, the other side held an assortment of textbooks, ranging from philosophy to psychology and books on political science.

Curiosity piqued, Dumby directed his attention towards the sole window adorning the office space. He briefly paused to observe a man, clad in thermal underwear, engaged in a heated dispute with two officers from the Buffalo Police Department. The man struggled to restrain his two headstrong German Shepherds, their energy yearning to break free in a swift sprint or perhaps even leap toward the officers. The officers, one hand resting on their unfastened holsters, extended their left hand to calm the man.

"Merci." Jean Pierre added, "Buffalo has a unique food culture that fills at all price points. I notice that food travelers immediately feel at home with the city, its food, and its people. Within just a week, Sylvie and I had great success in finding the best places to open restaurants in Buffalo."

"What kind?" Dumby inquired from where he stood next to the window.

"Well, monsieur Dumby, it features a chick setting with new technology ..."

"Sheek."

"Yes, pardon me, chic. We have introduced an extensive wine list, state-of-the-art small plates, a sophisticated ambience, and an eclectic menu of delicious dishes." Jean Pierre stopped and thought, "This once, Sylvie and I decided to..."

"I'm sure about the delicious part," Bilac bent frontward to adjust himself on the work chair. He pulled on his jacket lapels and settled back.

"Yeah, yes, Senator Bilac," Jean Pierre doesn't finish the idea Sylvie and he had in mind for their restaurants. "It's at the intersection of Cleveland Drive and Beach Road, the first thing you see as you exit the I-95 towards Cleveland Hills."

"We know," Both Hawks spoke at once.

Jean Pierre laughed sheepishly, "Of course, messieurs. Then you must have seen it also?"

Sylvie was quiet by her husband, observing the three men and their conversation.

"Nope, not yet," Dumby finally settled his weight on a chair, and as he talked, he straightened the stuff on the desk, ensuring everything was square and adequately spaced. There wasn't much, to begin with, a phone, a legal-sized lined yellow pad, a translucent Bic pen with a black top, and a big plastic empty picture frame.

Sylvie spoke for the first time since she entered the office, "We hired a professional French architect who creates a harmonious design by combining existing features of the structure with attention to detail in several key areas.

"We also hired a team of 3D special visual effects," he said. He looked at Dumby, who was now leaning back in the chair and cranked his neck hard over. He could see the sky from the office window: delft-blue, cloudless, and so bright, it looked solid.

Jean Pierre continued, "Great space planning is vital to a restaurant's success."

Bilac nodded, and Dumby moved his head back to its normal position on the neck.

"How much are you going make us spend?" Dumby was testing the waters.

"You told us money did not matter and that the sky was the limit?" Sylvie battened in an assertive voice, shooting from the hip.

"Yes, yes, Sylvie, of course," Dumby responded, adjusting his necktie, letting some steam off.

"Now that we have identified the target customers positively, we think we should feed the right ambiance. We could do this by selecting appropriate furnishing, color, lighting, and the cutlery design adapted to them."

"Uh huh?" Bilac humored Jean Pierre.

"Oui. Both restaurants are built from red bricks, with indoor pillars, overhead fluorescent bulbs, warm lighting, and wall-sized windows. With the low and warm lighting, they are very often romantic. We have put fresh flowers, tasteful artwork on the walls, classical music, linen tablecloths, and napkins," Sylvie replied.

"In the beginning, Sylvie and I s'agitaientover at the restaurant, arguing like two kids. However, we found a middle ground, and Mr. Sebastian Mateo, the architect, God bless him, helped us to déterminer a whole lot of factors that go into the ouvrir of the restaurant." Jean Pierre paused for a beat, then continued,

"We have that unique technical progrès, which will make you proud of me, us. Mr. Mateo chose colors that reflect both our taste. The seating is unique and considerably for the privileged to maximize profits by taste. How do you say, unrivaled, singular, unmatched, like Chez Jean Pierre Labaguette, the lighting fixtures reflect our French Class ..." He paused. "Is it correct to call it that?"

"Call it election manipulation, voter fraud, or vote rigging; it's all the same," Dumby said, clicking on the thrust device of the Bic pen as a force of habit. Bilac looked at him and then at the pen, making the 'clicking' noise and making Dumby stop. "Please continue."

"When clients enter my restaurant at Cleveland Hill, the Cherie Café, they feel like they are in the Paris Champs Elysees. The far wall has a large mantle dominating the center. On the mantle, we have an antique clock and pictures of musicians. In front of that shelf is an upright piano and stage for virtual reality..."

"Wait a second," Bilac's forehead creases. "You guys bought a freaking Grand?"

"Non, no, no, Senator, it's a spinet upright piano, nothing fancy. Sam, the piano player, handles it like his baby and creates beautiful mellow sounds from a...."

"Spectrum?" Bilac helped him out. "And what's all that about VR?

"VR?"

"Virtual reality."

Jean Pierre felt doltish. "It is a state-of-the-art system. It benefits group chanter. Social interaction strongly contributes to improvements in mental and physical health, but so does vocal interaction in an immersive virtual acoustic (VIIVA) system, allowing the user to take part in a group singing activity in 360-degree virtual reality. They could hear themselves in the recorded venue alongside the other singers.

Sylvie added, "and particularly to control social communication in real group singing activities."

"Oui, oui. Spectrum of French music, and that fluent the note in a rich and echoing way. The Cafê is always filled with sweet, round, dark, and rich sounds," JP noted.

Sylvie contributed further to the conversation, "Hanging on the wall above the piano are pictures of famous French singers Edith Piaf, Charles Aznavour, and Serge Gainsbourg.

"And we have virtual reality 3D of them. They will appear on the stage with their songs. We have secured the copyright rights"

"Can you imagine yourself having dinner and listening to Edith Piaf, the famous French singer, and she will look you in the eyes while she sings?"

Jean Pierre said, "Je ne regrette rien, ni le bien qu'on ma fait, ni le mal, tout cela m'est bien égal Si tu me le demandais, Je renierais ma patrie Je renierais mes amis Si tu me le demandais, On peut bien rire de moi, Je ferais n'importe quoi Si tu me le demandais."[15]

Or the other French icon, Charles Aznavour.

Je n'ai pas vu le temps courir Je n'ai pas entendu sonner Les heures de mon devenir Quand je fonçais tête baissée Vers ce qu'était un avenir Et qui est déjà du passé.

---

[15] "I don't regret anything, neither the good done to me, nor the bad, I don't care [9] If you asked me, I'd deny my country I'd deny my friends If you asked me, I could be laughed at, I'd do anything If you asked me."

Or Serge Gainsbourg. "Je t'aime, je t'aime Oh, oui, Je t'aime Moi non plus Oh, mon amour Comme la vague irrésolue Je vais, je vais et je viens Entre tes reins Je vais et Je viens Entre tes reins Et Je me retiens."[16]

Jean Pierre ignored Dumby and continued, "There is a double door, kinda bat-man doors, between the reception and the piano, which leads to the main dining area. Looking through the dining area wall windows is the Central Amherst Park Lake. This side of the door is my desk. It is a large walnut piece..."

"We get the idea, but it will need a large investment," Sylvie said. "Do you want to have the leader in French Cuisine?"

"This is Rich Cuisine"

Jean Pierre's face lit up as if he was waiting to be asked this, "The Provincial French Cooking to Nouvelle Cuisine, the ingredients can remain the same, made famous by just presenting them differently. Foie Gras is one of the most popular and well-known delicacies in French cuisine, and its flavor is described as rich, buttery, and delicate..."

Sylvie added, tetchily, "We have Truffles or Truffes in France. This is a group of valuable and highly sought-after edible underground fungi.

"Fungi? What the f...?" Dumby was disgusted.

"Hush, Dumby," Sylvie silenced Dumby to his contempt. "The most sought-after truffle is the Black truffle or Black Périgord Truffle. We also serve 'Cèpes,' one of France's most famous foods. These are wild mushrooms that are edible and

---

[16] "I love you; I love you... Oh, yes, I love you Me neither Oh, my love Like the irresolute wave I go, I go and I come Between your loins I go and I come Between your loins And I hold back.

growing all over the countryside in France. Then there are confits, which is a technique in preservation. Preserving meats has been important in the past due to the lack of refrigeration...."

JP then jumped in, "Roquefort Cheese is made from ewe's milk and comes from southern France. So, to speak from Roquefort-sur-Soulzon. Roquefort is rated as one of the world's greatest blue cheeses. Brie Cheese is perhaps one of the most famous of the 400-plus French cheeses in France. The original Brie-de-Meaux' comes from the smallest French province of France, Ile de France."

"Yes, yes, OK. That's enough," Bilac interjects, much to JP's disinclination.

"Alright, Oui."

"What about the other one?" Dumby queried.

"20 Walden Avenue."

"Not the address. We know where it is; we just told you. The name. What's the name of the damn place?" Dumby was getting impatient for some reason.

"That is the name of the restaurant, Mr. Dumby."

"Huh? Alright."

"Also designed by Mr. Sebastian Mateo, this time with a checkered-tiled floor and a minimalist approach. The brick and asphalt and neon are blurred by distance and sunshine beneath it. But in making these decisions, we always had to know that restaurant design is ultimately about creating an unforgettable and comfortable customer experience. When people talk about a restaurant's 'great vibe', they're talking about an experience that design choices have guided."

"We serve crab cooked in a vodka sauce, asparagus, and baby shell pasta. If you are a vegetarian, I recommend trying Walnuts. They are famous in the Perigord region of France. Walnut trees are grown all over the southeast area of France. They seem confined to the Dordogne valley and the countryside that borders it. Sweet Chestnuts are most famous in the Perigord region and surrounding areas. They were once the most important foodstuff in this area. Clafouti is possibly the most famous traditional dessert from southwest France. 'Le Clafouti' is traditionally made with wild cherries and comes from Limousin. And we thought we'd diversify a little with grilled asparagus, enjoy the delectable taste by ordering the pasta Martoche."

"JP, you were supposed to become American, not The Godfather!"

Jean Pierre waved his hand and smiled, "Don't worry, all your favorite dishes are also on the menu. We thought diversity was the new à la mode in fashion in America.

"Lovely, isn't it?" Bilac looked towards Dumby, who had his head resting on his arms on the table.

"Huh, what?" He had dozed off. He immediately wiped the drool off his face. "Yes, er, no... what? Sorry."

"Nothing."

Then, to Jean Pierre and Sylvie, he said, "Can we get you anything, coffee, pop..."

"I'm good, Merci," He knew what he would find: faded walls, a soda dispenser for breakfast, and a pair of potted palms clinging to life for the coffee maker to spill the beans.

"I'm gorgeous, OK," Sylvie concurred. She was in concession with her husband and did not want to have trash food.

"Great, then," Bilac exclaimed. "Let's get to the point, shall we?"

Dumby straightened to get up, pouring himself a glass of water from the dispenser as he said, "On cue."

"Alright, JP, here's the deal. We are looking for a presidential candidate, my friend. It could have been you; you are smart and express yourself well. You have a Creole wife, and your twin children are mixed races; therefore, we will get white and black votes."

"Our political program could be like a menu," Dumby added. "The only thing is that if you were not born in America, your birth certificate will be scrutinized by the Democrats. Sorry."

Jean Pierre remained remarkably composed despite being presented with the absurd strategy proposed by the two Hawks. "Ultimately, I have no desire to pursue the presidency. I appreciate the offer nonetheless," he calmly remarked, his demeanor betraying no hint of agitation or uncertainty.

"Yes, you will be Jean Pierre. This is your time, our time," replied Sylvie assertively.

He crossed his legs again, raising the left leg opening, stretched upwards towards the top seam, "You know what? I was born in America."

Jerry Bilac and Ted Dumby look at each other and then at Jean Pierre's raised trousers. "No socks?" Dumby proclaims.

Jean Pierre moves forward, slants his head a little, and looks down at his derby. "No? Why? What's wrong with?"

Bilac looked at Dumby again and shook his head slightly when JP was checking out his ankle region.

"I was born in South Carolina. My father was in the US Army. My mother is French; she was a famous cook."

Both Hawks looked at each other again; their eyes were animated, protractedly wide. "Yes, we can." They jumped from their seats and performed a square dance.

The room went completely silent, except for the clicking sound, indicating that the components of the centrally air-conditioned system were working just fine, and the whistling sound from a supply air vent when the volume was damp inside. Everything was working fine, even the selection of a French restaurateur as a candidate for the upcoming American elections.

****

5

Jean Pierre Youth

"The American dream does not come to those who fall asleep."

— Richard Nixon

1983: Flashback to the Childhood Memories of Our Future US President

About forty years ago, a pair of twins were to be born to an American French couple at the General Military Hospital (GMH) for the North Carolina Troops in the coastal town of Savannah, Virginia.

The mother was rushed to the GMH, which could be easily reached by employing an Ambulance Car, which Jean Pierre's father had called for when her water had broken, and the father had panicked. The ambulance carried the soon-to-be mother. It had sped across the city of Richmond.

Upon arriving, the mother-to-be, Mrs. Noémie Harris Labaguette (her mother 's maiden name, which she had decided to hold on to), was hurried to the labor room. She appeared chafed and exhausted, nearly on the brink of tears, while her tall, American-looking husband attempted to console her. The midwife administered medicines and employed other techniques to dilate the pregnant woman 's cervix, to induce contractions, and prepare her for a vaginal birth before the doctor arrived.

As soon as the nurse/midwife saw Doctor Edward James, she immediately briefed him about the woman who did not appear American despite her Caucasian appearance. "Doctor James, thank goodness you're here," she said as she looked at the ADPIE Progress Report and faced the doctor. "Labor is induced at term, with administration of dinoprostone topical."

"I'd suggest elective induction due to her discomfort and scheduling issues. Waiting any longer may lead to complications since we're dealing with twins. "Did you give her anything for the pain?"

"Systemic analgesics have been administered through an intravenous line."

"We do not know if elective labor induction will lead to higher or lower cesarean delivery rates than waiting for labor to start on its own."

"Cesarean!" Nurse Hatchett exclaimed.

"I've assessed the risk of cesarean delivery from the woman 's age. It is her first pregnancy, and the status of her cervix." he did not complete his statement. Instead, he said, "Elective induction does not appear to affect the health of the babies."

"Get ready for a cesarean," Doctor James alerted Nurse Hatchett. "Epidural block in the lower back. For labor and vaginal delivery, a combination of analgesics and anesthetics might have been required."

He went to the couple and spoke to them after greeting them. He looked at Noémie and said, "You will have some loss of feeling in the lower areas of your body, but you will remain awake and alert. You should be able to bear down and push your babies through the birth canal. The reason why you will lose sensation is because "for cesarean delivery, the dose of anesthetic may have to be increased. This may cause a loss of sensation in the lower half of your body. "

"Qu'a-t-il dit exactement?" [17] Noémie had asked her husband. Although enigmatic, she was drained of all color. Noémie was discreet, diverse, and incredibly subtle. She wasn't too flashy and cool with imperfections. Noémie had messy, 'just-woke-up-like-this' hair, which was initially a Françoise Hardy-style fringes, with natural, less-is-more makeup; the mascara rolled down her face, as tears prattled out of her eyes out of pain.

On a regular day, her looks were absorbed as a form of disregard, and that freedom of being was probably what people found attractive. She was a natural beauty.

---

[17] "What did he say?"

The husband explained what the doctor had just said to her lovely and dissipated wife. Just like Sylvie, Noémie's English was superficial at best. He spoke to her in French, "méthodes de retardement ou d'induction du travail." [18] To the doctor, he said, "Excuse me. doctor..."

"James, Doctor Edward James."

"Yes, Doctor James, can you please tell me about the possible harms and benefits for both the mother and babies, such as the risk of c-section and the risk of low birth weight? I want to be sure about the risks."

"We need to hurry, sir. Don't worry. She's in good hands," He announced as he looked back at him as they shifted Noémie to another room. "You may come with us if you want."

****

The twin father Sergeant Jonathan Harris, a thirty-three-year-old American man, was five foot nine inches. He was a large man, just shy of being overweight—average Jonathan had gotten used to having his age mistaken for ten years younger than he was.

He had waited outside, and as soon as Nurse Hatchett had come running out of the labor room, she was out of breath but managed to tell him that his lovely wife. Mrs. Noémie Harris Labaguette had given birth to a pair of healthy twins.

"Vigorous Twins? Oh my God."

Overjoyed and unglued at hearing this, he first asked about

---

[18] "Methods for delaying or inducing labor."

his wife and if he could see her. They let him meet her as Noémie lay on a hospital bed with the side railings down and the headrest inclined. Mrs. Noémie Harris Labaguette held one baby in each arm. She smiled when she saw her husband, "On a eu des beaux jumeaux, tu sais?" [19]

"Oui," he drew closer. They're beautiful. Il suffit de les regarder, ils sont beaux." [20]He extended his hands, picked one of them up and kept looking at the tiny boy. He returned the first one and held the next little guy, "HÉ le bel homme."[21]

Jonathan raised his voice for everyone to hear, "My son John Peter and Peter John will be military like me."

"Non-Monsieur c'est Jean Pierre et Pierre Jean et ils seront cuisiniers comme moi," [22] Noémie had proudly said with authority as she looked at the returned baby.

After returning home to their house in the Windsor Lake apartments in Virginia Beach, the couple found themselves at odds with each other just two days into their new life.

Welcoming a new baby, or in this case, babies, is usually an exhilarating event, especially for first-time parents. But it also brings a whole array of new challenges to their relationship. Despite being adorable and lovable, newborns can be quite demanding. Even the most well-prepared couples often feel exhausted and stretched thin during those initial months. It's no wonder that many find themselves engaging in more frequent

---

[19] "We had twins, you know?"
[20] "Just look at those, they are beautiful."
[21] "Hey handsome..."
[22] "Non-Monsieur, it is Jean Pierre and Pierre Jean, and they will be cooks like me."

arguments.

This became extremely frustrating and worrying for Jonathan and Noémie, especially when they assumed and firmly believed the babies would bring them closer together. This kept escalating to a point where Noémie wanted to return to her village on the northwestern outskirts of Paris, France. The town was located thirty kilometers from the center of Paris. She went to the village to live with her family and helped with the business. Noémie's family was supportive of her small private enterprise, a restaurant, "The Restaurant Les Jumeaux."

Noémie spent a long time in France. However, she had not divorced Jonathan, well, not yet, and it had been a few years since she had moved back. The twins had grown up, and the two boys helped their mother run the place.

Between March 2003 and January 2014, the trio successfully managed the restaurant, which thrived by catering to the local community and the occasional tourists who likely stumbled upon its inviting ambiance. The inference behind this was: "We are lost anyway, so we might as well eat something, even if it tastes like codfish."

Nonetheless, codfish and semen or no codfish and semen, the restaurant progressed well – despite today's special: 'Codfish & Semen, with Truffles, Fleur de sel, Dijon mustard, and of course Olive pie –the Labaguette family was happy and self-sufficient.

"Pourquoi ne retournes-tu pas en Amérique."[23] Her mother had asked once, "Jonathan est seul et ne s'est pas marié[24]. She

---

[23] "Why don't you go back to America?"
[24] "is alone and has not married."

had said looking Noémie in her dark deep-set eyes. "He has not even seen the baby boys?"

"Oui, je sais que cela semble fou pour quelqu'un peut-être qui n'a pas été là bas."[25] She added, "bien qu'il y aura des problèmes et des difficultés dans l'année à venir, dès mon retour."[26]

Her mother had shaken her head and sighed while she ruffled the hair of the two young boys.

Present Day

Four people sat in a room at the GOP headquarters: Sylvie, Jean Pierre, Senator Bilac, and Republican Dumby. The room was utterly silent at one point. Sylvie, a strong, elegant French businesswoman, kept clarifying and illustrating the menu at the restaurants they recently opened.

"Black Truffle Soup, with beef broth, vegetables, black truffles, puff pastry; Spring Garlic Soup, seasoned with fiddlehead ferns and foraged mushrooms; Grilled Asparagus, frisée, poached egg, tomato confit, sherry wine vinaigrette; Smoked Salmon, with crème fraîche, panna cotta, buckwheat blini, trout caviar; Grilled Octopus cooked with English peas, torpedo onions, laratte potatoes, Provencal oil; Roasted Baby Beets; Seasonal Salad; House-made Charcuterie, condiments, pickles, chutney; Chef's Choice Fromage with fig compote, smoked almonds; Roasted East Coast Oysters; Spring Pea Jean Pierre; Crispy Tofu and Mushrooms; Guinea Foul; - then comes the second course...."

---

[25] "Yes, I know it sounds crazy for someone maybe who hasn't been there."
[26] "There will be problems as soon as I return."

"Yes, all right, Sylvie, we get the idea," Bilac was getting impatient.

Sylvie paid him no attention and went on. "Crispy Dorade; Market Fish; Pork Tenderloin Duck Breast..."

"Yes, Sylvie, that's amazing. You have our full support," Dumby told her.

Sylvie pretended not to have heard Dumby again and kept going. "Blackberry sorbet, shortbread, aged balsamic; Desserts Du Marché, with crêpe, cake, mascarpone cream cherry clafouti smoked chocolate beignet; then we have Gâteau Au Chocolat..."

"That's enough!" Bilac finally lost control and shouted as Sylvie and JP looked at him with displeasure and annoyance. Their fragile, sore egos had been hurt, and you may have heard the idiom, 'hell hath no fury as an uptight, upper lip, bourgeoise, pompous, conceited, narcissistic, egomaniacal Gallic couple scorned.'

"You can't talk to my wife like that, Senator Bilac."

"You're right, I'm sorry." The gasbag 's repetitive and utterly useless blabber had left Bilac feeling distracted and annoyed. In a momentary lapse of diplomacy, he lashed out at Sylvie when she wouldn't stop talking about French cuisine. Deep down, he hoped that the couple hadn't been offended. He wouldn't have thrown her, or her contemptuous, autocratic biggety of a husband, had the stakes not been set this high.

He felt extorted, coerced, and abused. Somewhere deep inside, he had begun to lament this whole laughable animus. He wasn't sure, but they had already given the French couple so much money and funded their portfolio of establishments in the US. Besides, the greedy couple would not return a cent of it if plans changed. Therefore, he simply apologized and let the world move on with blinders and a white stick and a nitwit Jew bag system of a French cook as a potential candidate for the American Presidency.

The irony!

"What the heck was I thinking?" Dumby thought.

****

After showing his birth certificate from South Carolina to Ted and Jerry, they both exclaimed in disbelief. "You are an American."

He shook his head and smiled, looking at the authoritative chameleons. "As I mentioned, "My father was in the US Army. My mother is French; she was a famous cook in France."

"Here we go again," Bilac thought, raising one hand to his forehead and rubbing his temple. "we're now stuck between Scylla and Charybdis. All these people have on their doltish minds is food."

He said, "My brother and I helped her with the restaurant before I shifted to the US and Pierre Jean est resté derrière [27] with my mother."

Dumby and Bilac looked at each other, and they shook their heads in an attempt to convey a lack of interest as if trying to say, "What the heck have we gotten ourselves into?" If only Sylvie and JP might provide a way out of the taedium vitae that formed

---

[27] "Stayed back."

their spiritual landscape.

"That's great, JP. Good to know," Bilac interfered. "Knowing that you're American has solved half our problems."

"Excuse me?"

"The current president stunned the political world in 2016 when he became the first person without government or military experience ever to be elected president of the United States. His four-year tenure in the White House revealed extraordinary fissures in American society but left little doubt that he is a figure unlike any other in the nation's history." Dumby said.

"John Barron's policy record included major changes at home and abroad," Bilac added.

"I moved back to the USA ten years ago. I do not want to change my French restaurant into a kebab between the rise of the Muslim culture and the rise of the French taxes; my choice was easy," Jean Pierre said calmly.

"Now, easy tiger, no hate spee..."

"Qui se soucie des Musulmans?"[28]

Ted Dumby and Jerry Bilac had the same thing in their minds, and Dumby spoke for them both, "Can you do us a favor?

"Ouvrir un restaurant à la Maison Blanche?"[29] JP said, mockingly.

Sylvie laughed heartily.

---

[28] "Who cares about Muslims?"
[29] "Open a restaurant in the White House?"

"What was that?" Bilac asked.

"Nothing. You were saying?"

"We'd like you to prepare a political speech as you present a menu and show it to us. Can you do that, Jean Pierre?" Dumby asked JP.

"Give me a week," Jean Pierre said as he opened a suitcase and gave them some pastries. "Here you go. Try these."

They taste the pastries.

"My goodness, if his speech is as good as his pastries, the Democrats are fucked!" Jerry exclaimed.

****

6

Political Ascension of Jean Pierre

Aristocracy is the spirit of the Old Testament, democracy of the New."

— **Napoleon**

The Republican headquarters buzzed with activity. A sea of people looked like a big dollop of suits hurrying to meet deadlines. Margarette Cobblepot observed the activity from her place behind the reception desk of the GOP Headquarters. All along, Margarette had ridden with the punches.

She had changed her hairstyle to look more French and was wearing a Chinese copy of a "Channel "tailleur.""

Ms. Cobblepot's sensation of being overwhelmed by the crowd was akin to a raindrop attempting to resist joining the vast ocean. However, Margarette, the raindrop in question, ultimately fused with the collective body politic, albeit reluctantly. The surging energy coursed through her being, causing her to envision the very foundation quivering beneath her feet. She found great delight in this evocative experience, as it served as a poignant reminder of the futility and emptiness prevalent within the corridors of power. It made her feel significant in a world where people, especially the proletarians and those with pink-collar jobs, were dismissed left, right, and center.

"That outfit makes you look more hourglass-shaped," Dumby said with a smile, which wasn't innocent at all as he ogled her generous cleavage with utmost concentration and lust, preferential to politicians his age and status.

Despite her repulsion, she possessed enough intelligence to perceive it as a backhanded compliment, regardless of her personal preferences. It implied the act of crafting a deceptive facade, suggesting that she appeared thinner than her actual physique.

She unexpectedly caught a glimpse of Gilbert Mathews, the tall member of Senator Bilac's staff of German descent.

She stood on her toes and moved her head from side to side. Looking through the mob, she called him, "Gilbert, hey Gil!"

He turned and bumped into a lady. He excused himself and looked for the owner of the voice.

"Here, Gil, Margarette," she spoke as she raised her arm and waved.

He saw her and elbowed his way to her, "Hey, Maggie, you look like a French fashion magazine woman. What a nice change."

"Hello." Her fondness for him was evident as a faint blush colored her cheeks, prompted by his proximity. Only the reception desk stood between them, mere inches apart. "The Labaguettes are expected today. Senator Jerry Bilac asked me to ensure everyone was present, including you."

"Yes, I received a message from Ted Dumby." I'm waiting for them to walk in through the door." He looked back, and the lobby appeared less congested.

"Great. Let me know if you guys need anything."

****

A few hours later, Jean Pierre, Sylvie, Ted Dumby, and Jerry Bilac were joined by speech writer Gloria Winston, who was trying to analyze the voice and tone of Jean Pierre and Sylvie to prepare a speech best suited to them.

A Caucasian man of average height in his twenties entered the room a little while later. He had a Blackmagic Ursa Mini Pro 12K professional camera hanging from one shoulder. His hair was tied in a ponytail, and he wore jeans, a simple tee, and a round-neck sweater. He had put on a pair of Nike Air.

"I'm sorry, I'm late. Hi, I'm Peter Silas," Delicately, he set his camera on the table and tidied himself up. He brushed his hair away from his forehead, undoing the ponytail before deftly tying it back into a fresh one. He observed the array of individuals in the room with a red scrunchie clenched between his teeth. "The security checks retained me, the registered private security agents carried out." He looked as if trying to recall something and continued, "That's what you guys call them, right? They took forever with the camera and the frisking."

"It doesn't matter what we call them. Is that thing rolling?" Bilac pointed to the Blackmagic Ursa.

"No, but it will once you tell me."

"All right, wait."

Bilac nodded towards Evans, prompting the cameraman to commence filming. Jean Pierre had a penchant for effortlessly stylish ensembles like her male counterpart. He donned an unironed, button-down shirt in a neutral hue, complemented by a Dior Men's Cotton V Neck Sweater. The shirt's collars were neatly tucked into the V-neck of the sweater. Completing the ensemble, he sported well-fitted slacks and a timeless black belt. His feet were ornamented with Christian Louboutin shoes and a Bleu Nero Luxurious looped scarf for an ultra-Parisian look. "Yes, yes, very much so."

The first thing the Americans noticed about Sylvie was her dress style. They remained mesmerized by her ability to seamlessly blend simplicity with profoundness, creating an effortlessly minimalist style. They couldn't help but notice the fusion of timeless aesthetics with a relaxed and effortless vibe, resulting in a natural, undone yet remarkably sophisticated appearance.

"A plain white buttoned-down shirt is an absolute must for

me," Sylvie said when she figured out what the cameraman was here for. "Whether you are pairing it with a simple slip skirt or favorite straight-leg jeans, this layering piece is a French staple." She wore a structured blazer over the Rouge shirt, a simple gold necklace, high-rise straight-leg jeans by Gap, and a pair of Escarpin Louis Vuitton. She carried a handbag with her, which she had placed on the table. It was a bag "over the moon."

"All right. Peter. Take a cue."

"Yeah?" The cameraman responded to Dumby.

"Please sit with Gloria," he pointed to her, thinking he might go and sit with Sylvie, "Take notes of the angles and the theme we want to project."

Gloria shifted in her chair, "Yes, I have the game plan for you, Peter...?"

"Silas."

"Mr. Silas..."

"Call me Pete."

As he approached Gloria, she handed him a piece of paper. He looked at it intensively.

"Jean Pierre, how about we get down to business?"

"All your senator."

"Great," he looked at Dumby and said, "You ready?"

Dumby nodded.

"Let's get this show on the road— we're running a ducky. The freaking Doves somehow have an idea of what's happening here."

"How?" Dumby was genuinely concerned.

"Never mind that. It's hall'n oats from now on."

****

The following week, Jean, Sylvie, Bilac, and Dumby gathered at the republican office to discuss the campaign.

"In short, the earlier we start campaigning, the better. The best politicians always manage their distributed organizing campaigns, if only in their heads."

"What's distributed organizing campaigns?" Sylvie asked.

"It is a community organizing strategy that prioritizes the work being done by subsets or chapters of the central organization. It is set up to take advantage of the superior campaigning power of local people rather than regional or national ones."

"Spank me if I can understand words of what you say," Jean Pierre remarked.

The Senator continued, "This is done through building relationships, figuring out our future campaign stance, based on the outcome, or what the word on the streets is, and so on. However, if we are discussing your upcoming election, we want to start assembling your team and figuring out your campaign strategy as early as possible. All your campaign elements, like donations, the number of campaign team members, voters contacted, etc., will benefit from a longer lead time."

"Ça me va, car j'aime notre nouvelle routine," [30] Sylvie

---

[30] "It's fine with me because I like our new routine."

71

looked at Jean Pierre as she spoke.

"Excuse me?" Dumby sounded annoyed. "English, please, have some courtesy, Sylvie."

"Alright, alright, okay?" Jean Pierre raised his voice, and his face became flushed. He got up from his chair and firmly placed his hands on the table. "Mr. Dumby, please understand that we are French. We are a sophisticated breed to all other nations."

"That's better," Dumby said.

"Please understand, JP, you're running for the most powerful position in the world. Speak in Greek if you wish, and goddam me if I complain. And I know your English is so good, it makes me wonder why you must speak French. Well, it's your call; you'll be the boss of everyone and everything in a few, so speak French all you want."

"Yes, I want to focus on English as the main international language, anyway,"

"You're right, JP, absolutely correct! One hundred per cent!" Bilac moved his upper body forward. "He knew a rather scathing response would not allow JP to get a whiff of, being the..." His thoughts were interrupted by JP.

"That's like a good do... man. Sylvie says it sounds good because she's fond of our new arrangement." Jean Pierre interjected.

"What?"

"She's fond of it," Bilac clarified boorishly.

"Ah. Well, in that case, there's more," Dumby said as he got off his chair and walked to the window.

"What have we been cooking now, Mr. Ted?"

"Firstly, it is no surprise that traditional organizing over large areas or diverse memberships suffers from disconnection in communication; this means we need to overcome that by having communication systems in place...Are you filming this, Peter?"

"No, er, yeah," Peter turned the camera to Dumby.

"Get it away from me. Focus on the Labaguettes," Dumby said, again turning his gaze to stare out the window.

Senator Bilac continued, "Secondly, it is clear that there is a declining return for organizations that depend on email communication, social media advertising, clicktivism, and so on...."

"What about the printing and newspapers and wall posters?" Jean Pierre asked, raising his left eyebrow.

"In-depth interviews and survey evidence from none other than the French and also the Dove party members are used to show the presence of posters in elections, which is primarily intended to signal the strength of the party's campaign."

"And we will be doing that, starting today, after you've selected the picture that goes on print media," Dumby said.

"What photo?" JP asked.

"Peter, please click a few stills of the couple and their children and then Jean Pierre alone?"

"I don't think I understand, Senator Bilac."

"Haven't I introduced our French friends to you?"

Peter shakes his head.'

Reluctantly, Bilac proceeded to introduce the couple to Peter, emphasizing their refined elegance and impeccable manners. Despite his reservations, he felt compelled to do so. However, given the current chaos and conflict surrounding the Hawks, he immediately regretted ever crossing paths with the French couple. "We want the final pictures to make them look like movie stars! Celebrities, Sorry, I mean superstars of this blue planet."

Peter looks at Bilac and then at the couple, "You got it, Senator."

Bilac started from where he had been interrupted by Jean Pierre, "Minor parties use them to inform the public."

"Okay," Jean Pierre shook his head before giving Bilac a thumbs up with a shit-eating grin on his long face. "Les doigts dans le nez!"[31]

Bilac looked at Jean Pierre, "I could cut off that bloody Cyrano de Bergerac nose." Then, again, "Does he even understand what I'm saying to him, that French clown tool?" – continued. "Finally, and this doesn't cover everything by any means, the distributed organizing must be truly scalable. Once two or three chapters have been set up and functioning independently, it can scale quickly to twenty or 200 chapters."

The Labaguettes appeared perplexed and disoriented, unable to comprehend a single word of what Bilac and Dumby were saying. Nonetheless, they continued nodding in an attempt to avoid appearing foolish. However, unbeknownst to them, their attempts to save face fell flat. They not only resembled clueless individuals but rather resembled donuts

---

[31] "Fingers in the nose!"

attending an extravagant costume party. Then someone knocked on the door.

"Yeah?" Dumby raised his voice.

"This is campaign specialist Gilbert Mathews."

"Come in."

"Hello…"

"You're late," Bilac gave him a dirty look.

He didn't respond and sat on a chair next to the to-be power couple, "Hi, I'm Gilbert. You must be Jean Pierre and Sylvie."

"Yes, that's what we are," Sylvie smiled. JP looked at him and back to Bilac.

"Women have been voting for nearly 100 years. Why stop now?" Dumby took a political campaign poster from his suitcase for the 'get out the vote (GOTV) poster. "For instance, this encourages women to vote even today, in a few but powerful words." He paused to think and continued. "Let's talk about beam-time."

"About whose?" Sylvie asks.

"Airwaves, live broadcasts, the television?"

"Okay, okay."

"You sure, Sylvie? Do you understand any of this?"

"Il ne faut pas pousser Mamie dans les orties!" JP said to Dumby.

"…Surtout si elle n'a pas de culotte! [32] "Sylvie added,

_____

[32] "Especially if she has no panties!"

snickering.

"Et Pourquoi ça?"[33] JP glared at his wife with anger evident in his gaze. In response, she met his gaze, rolled her eyes, and shifted uncomfortably in her chair.

"All right, guys, enough, please. We don't have all day," Bilac tried to sound authoritative.

"Go ahead. Nobody's in your way," JP said.

Bilac shook his head very slightly, barely noticeable, and continued, "In 1952, Nixon, faced with a potential scandal, made what must have seemed like a radical decision. He decided to address the nation on television. Richard Nixon wasn't running for president yet. Nixon's address was a Hail Mary attempt to keep his spot on the Republican ticket with nominee Dwight Eisenhower in the wake of a major scandal. Nixon would have his problems with TV later. Still, the Checker speech secured the future of his political career and marked a change in the way American politicians would campaign going forward.

"Believe it or not, there was a time in American politics when it was seen as uncouth for presidential candidates to campaign. They might make some public addresses at campaign rallies, but for the most part, they left the campaigning to the political parties and their staffs."

"Okay. I think I'm getting an idea. They are a clever way to advertise and promote mine and your political ideas. inscrutable."

"Ours," Bilac emphasizes.

---

[33] "And why is that?"

"Huh?"

"You said yours and...."

"Oh, oh no, I mean, oh yes, ours, hours, le nôtre. I have got the ideas."

"You have, er, you are Jean Pierre, getting an idea?" Bilac leaned in, "That's wonderful." He glared at the French lady, "How about you, Sylvie?"

"I'm fine, just keep my, er, marri, ummm... Mon mari m'a demandé de bouger prudemment."[34]

"She's saying I've asked her to be all ears, eyes, and brains."

"And booty," Dumby looked out the window.

"What?"

"I said 'goody'... Good job, JP," He turned to smile, and all the Americans in the room looked at him with a hint of a smile about to crack some mouths.

Dumby shrugged, not saying anything.

Jean Pierre waved his hand, "Ah, it is not a thing."

****

Two days and a campaign slogan later, the French couple graced the national television screens, accompanied by their delightful children—a boy and a girl—who shared an uncanny resemblance to Jean Pierre. Patrick, the boy, possessed a darker complexion compared to his sister Jacqueline. The family appeared impeccably attired, holding hands and radiating an

---

[34] "My husband has asked me to tread carefully."

aura of perfection. Major networks dedicated extensive coverage to the French couple, ensuring their presence shone brightly at the Buffalo Hilton. Camera flashes illuminated the Hilton Garden Inn, causing it to shimmer with brilliance. All media outlets converged on the event, including CNN and BBC, Al-Jazeera, Fox, MSNBC, and numerous others.

The French couple exuded elegance and sophistication, skillfully adorning themselves with sparkling accessories and luxurious attire. Their eloquent speech left a sense of exoticism and refinement, with every syllable enunciated with precision. The faces of the couple adorned billboards and structures across prominent locations in New York City, New Jersey, and Connecticut, ensuring widespread visibility. The Labaguettes, particularly Jean Pierre, would soon find their faces adorning walls and structures in every city, courtesy of the promised efforts of the PR agency.

Jean Pierre raised his hand and could be heard on television, "John F. Kennedy says, let us resolve to be masters, not the victims, of our history." He paused and looked down at the podium to his notes. He read something written in French, 'contrôlant Notre proper destiny and remembered. He continued, "controlling our destiny without giving way to blind suspicions and emotions."

Later in the day, after meeting only a select few from the press and letting Dumby and the senator deal with complicated questions, Jean Pierre and Sylvie found themselves alone, far from the madding crowd, in a hallway south of the main auditorium of The Hilton. The last thing that JP heard was Dumby saying something about a press conference later that week to the reporters and that all their questions would be addressed then.

"Je perds la boule à présent," Jean Pierre said to his wife.

She hugged JP, gently pushed him away, stretched her arms, and curled her hands around his upper arms, "Ne t'inquiète pas."

He looked into her deep eyes and felt a little relaxed. Her eyes would always affect our man, "j'ai peur, c'est tout."

Sylvie drew him close again, "tu laisses la Grande Peur te dévorer, et ce n'est pas la Révolution française."

"Je sais."

"Alors?"

"J'ai peur de déclencher une révolution américaine."

"Oh, ne vous inquiétez pas alors," Sylvie smiled. "ces Américains aiment une bonne révolution."[35]

"But normally in another country," added Jean Pierre.

****

They are an instant hit with the Cowboys and their female counterparts. The nature of political news, mainly how the couple was filmed, as presented by the mass media in the

---

[35] "I'm losing my mind here."
"No, you're not."
"I'm just scared, is all."
"You're letting the Great Fear eat you whole; this isn't the French Revolution."
"I know."
"Then?"
"I'm scared of starting an American Revolution."
"Don't worry then; these Americans love a good revolution."

modern United States, affected people's emotional reactions more than their cognitive evaluations of political actors and institutions. The men adored Sylvie because of her gorgeous looks, sumptuous gym-body, and fashion sense.

Individuals who heavily depended on electronic media as their primary news source and consumed substantial amounts of mass media news tended to hold a favorable perception of Jean Pierre and Sylvie. Their response to the French couple was marked by positive emotional reactions, signifying an initial triumph for the Republicans. Jean Pierre's charming accent particularly smote women, while men were captivated by Sylvie's stunning and vibrant presence.

The American audience, which primarily obtained their news from television or radio, reacted similarly to those who mainly received news from newspapers. Sylvie's beauty enchanted even those. The French couple was widely exposed to the news, and America fell in love with them. Contrary to positive emotional reactions, the scenario differs regarding emotional responses. Individuals who primarily rely on television and radio for news consumption, coupled with high exposure to news content, tend to experience significantly more negative emotions than those who rely on newspapers and have limited exposure to news. However, here it was the complete opposite, with an entire nation enchanted by the spell the couple had cast over them with the help of Georgia and Peter.

7

The Campaign

"The future doesn't belong to the fainthearted; it belongs to the brave."

— Ronald Reagan

Two hundred eighty-nine miles away, at 671 Seneca St, Buffalo, in the Office building of the Erie County Democratic Committee, a few Doves gathered around the SONY LCD installed on the conference room wall.

"What the hell is this?" A man inquired, rather upset.

"An instruction manual on how to hand over America to France, in a silver platter, with a silk ribbon tied around it," another man said.

The lady responded, "Or, the Hawks have gone completely bonkers, and this is some kind of elaborate joke, something like what they did with Blondie, a TV personality, for heaven's sake!"

"Don't forget Reagan and what happened in 1962 and then in 1981."

"That was also the Republicans."

"Who is the foreigner?"

"Jean Pierre Labaguette."

"Who's the pin-up girl?"

"His wife, Sylvie. You must agree she has a great body. Look at those jugs on her and that junk in the fancy trunk. Man, she's a fire hazard."

The lady interjected, "You guys are obnoxious little runts. Have some respect."

"How long have you been watching this shit?"

"Did he say something about Libertarianism? Or did he mention anything about giving those the undermining influence? How about current inequalities in income and wealth or the value of political equality?"

"Nope. Most of Jean Pierre's speech was about how Washington reminded him of Paris and California vineyards reminded him of Bordeaux."

"They're not even close; they're bloody French. My

goodness!"

"Here comes the 'Freedom Fries' and Royale with Cheese against Le Big Mac."

James Bullard, the CEO of the Federal Reserve Bank of St. Louis, with the mighty Jay Leno chin and dull blue eyes, was the only one who had been silent since the conversation began until now. "Any preferences about raising the policy rate and the French man's views on predicting recession? Anything about the Federal Reserve partaking of a virtual European Economic and Financial Centre discussion?"

"None, no, not, zero, useless."

"Hmmm," Bullard looked at Samuel Peterson, a deliberative democrat and a long-term Secretary of Veterans Affairs currently serving as an attorney general for the democrats, who looked back with a pair of close-set, narrow green eyes with a twinkle in them. The attorney was good-looking, clean-shaven, and rugged with craggy skin. He sported a crew cut and often said it reminded him of his days in Saigon. His mouth curved into a smile, his forehead creased into a furrowed brow, and his upper lip curled into a grimace.

"They've gone mad. The term democratic competence has been stretched almost to the point of uselessness, and now we find ourselves under the guillotine," Attorney General Samuel Peterson continued. "This constant adding of desired traits – many of which are ideologically driven – misdirects efforts away from complex problems as the relationship between individual attributes and collective capacities."

"It was axiomatic until an hour ago," James Bullard said.

"What was?"

"That democracy cannot exist amid a citizenry incapable of executing its conditions," he took a sip from the Evian bottle. "This," he gestured towards the television with his right hand, with the water bottle still in his hand. "This is the final nail on the democratic coffin, and that French clown and the Hawks behind him are hellbent on proving that democracy is at best incapable."

Peterson added to what Bullard had to say, "If the dismal lessons of exporting democratic infrastructure from Europe taught us anything, it's that institutional reforms fail miserably without a receptive populace." His gaze shifted towards Clara Mayfield, a Congresswoman hailing from Milwaukee, aged thirty-nine. Clara was known for her consistent attire, often opting for a grey or black business suit. She kept her makeup minimal, relying on a subtle touch of lipstick in a light shade. With her shoulder-length hair, she exuded an air of professionalism and business acumen.

Her co-workers had thought she was a dyke for the longest time, but she had two kids from two different men. Sam sternly said to her, "Find something about him, tax evasions, infidelity, alcoholism, he is French, he must have a past, we can't let this happen – look at that herd of dumb people, believing a French man can run this country!"

"Well... Can an American?"

"Screw you. I want his birth certificate to be scrutinized under a microscope. I don't trust this Frenchman!"

"And they want him to be the president?"

"Of the United States, yes. You have a problem with that?"

The room went silent.

****

After a week, Clara returned. "Nothing, this guy is clean, but he has a twin brother in jail in France."

"Anything else?"

"Just put the TV on!"

When they switched it on, almost all news channels displayed the slogan that the Hawks came up with for Jean Pierre's campaign, "Something's Cooking in the Annals of Power, and it Smells Tantalizing!"

Sam put a hand to his head, shook it with his eyes shut tight, and his lips curled with rage, "Such bull!"

8

The Election

"We must dare to be great; and we must realize that greatness is the fruit of toil and sacrifice and high courage."

— Teddy Roosevelt

It was a victory celebration without much of a true heart-to-heart victory. Jean Pierre Labaguette was elected by a majority, a whopping seventy-six per cent.

The East Room of the White House showcased a scene of discarded wine glasses strewn across the table. Quiche Lorraine boxes and cans of Perrier were scattered throughout other areas of the complex. Meanwhile, the United States Capitol witnessed an abundance of champagne, flowing freely like water, as the Republicans indulged in joyous celebrations following Jean Pierre's victorious triumph over his Democratic rival.

Jean Pierre's win in the presidential election sparked impromptu street celebrations around the country on Saturday. Within seconds of the race being called, a crowd outside 315 State Street Albany, Buffalo, erupted in cheers. The festivities that continued all night brought some respite from the hectic schedule the Republicans had been hustling with for the last few months. A few bottles of the bubbly also helped break life's monotony.

"Is that Chateau Lafite 1869?" Sylvie asked, looking at the bottle with wide eyes.

"Yes, Sylvie, First Lady, that is certainly a bottle of Chateau Lafite 1869," Dumby said. "Ee also have Shipwrecked 1907 Heidsieck and Ampoule from Penfolds."

He turned his head and looked at a waiter in a uniform, a white shirt, and a black vest, with black trousers and dress shoes.

"Excuse me." Dumby squinted to read the name of the man's nameplate. "Jeremy?"

"Yes, Mr. Dumby, how can I be of service?"

"Can you bring in the Jesus Juice, the exclusive ones... Er, the space bags we...."

"Yes, certainly, sir." Jeremy smiled as he interjected before Dumby could finish. "Would you prefer the 1907 Heidsieck or the Chateau Lafite?"

"Get us anything older than a hundred years."

"Of course, and how about more than a 100-year-old?"

"We have those?"

"Yes, we do. The Chateau Lafite dates back to 1869." Jeremy said, "Located in Pauillac in the Médoc wine region, Château Lafite-Rothschild is a world-renowned winery with 1869 recognized as a top vintage produced by the Rothschild family."

"How do you...?"

Jeremy did not let Dumby interfere with his detailed account; for you see, Jeremy Richards was a wine specialist at the Mark Hotel in New York before he joined as a waiter and the Whitehouse kitchen assemblage in 2019, and when he spoke about wine.

"In 2010, three bottles of this vintage were each sold by Sotheby's in Hong Kong for US$232,000. The gravel from the nearby Gironde River creates the optimal conditions for the cabernet sauvignon grape variety to ripen, producing some of the best high-quality red wines on the planet."

"What, what, what?" Dumby shook his head. Just get the damn expensive Satan's urine."

Jeremy nodded. "There's also Chateau Lafite 1787, discovered in Paris among other wines from top vineyards, including Lafite. Etched into the unlabeled bottle was the year '1787', 'Lafitte,' and the initials 'ThJ.' Despite the aged appearance of the vessel, the wine itself was reported to be of high quality, with the engravings from eighteenth-century France, according to glass experts from Christie's. It is believed that the bottle once belonged to Thomas Jefferson, who developed a taste for French wine while serving as America's

Minister to France...."

"Thomas Jefferson? Wasn't he one of the presidents of the United States?" Sylvie asked Dumby.

"Yes, he was." Then to Jeremy, "Listen, man, just get us something. I'm parched."

"He was friendly with French people?"

"I wouldn't know, Sylvie, but the man sure loved his wine."

"I'll be right back with your drinks," Jeremy said as he walked away.

Dumby eyed Jeremy and nodded, "Where're Bilac and Jean Pierre?" He looked at Sylvie. At once, he felt desire take over him. He wanted to tell her that she was enticing. After all, her very presence would draw in men effortlessly. He tried to tell her that she was alluring as he felt her sexiness attracting and luring him to her.

"Sylvie."

"Yeah?"

"You are sensuous."

"Did you say anything?" Sylvie asked Dumby, with her forehead creased into a half frown.

"Who? Me?" He looked to his left and then to his right. He shrugged, "No, I was only wondering where our new President and the V.P. are."

"What is V.P.?

"Bilac, ex-Senator Jerry Bilac. That's what a V.P. is." As soon as he finished saying this, he saw them walking towards them from the far end of the vast hall. Their smiles were from ear to ear, and Jean Pierre had an eager bounce in his stride.

****

In other parts of the country, chants of "USA" broke out, "This is what democracy looks like." One woman popped a bottle of champagne and sprayed it over the crowd.

On an unseasonably mild November day in New York City, residents spilled out of their homes to revel in the streets. The jubilant atmosphere resonated across iconic locations such as Grand Army Plaza, Columbus Circle, Washington Square Park, and near Brooklyn's Fort Greene Park, where cheers erupted to celebrate Jean Pierre's momentous victory.

Times Square became a focal point for a massive gathering. At the same time, in various neighborhoods, the honking of car horns harmonized with the enthusiastic applause and cheers of pedestrians lining the sidewalks. The streets echoed with the chants of "Vive Jean-Pierre" as men, women, and children joined together to commemorate the ascension of Jean Pierre to the presidency of the United States.

"This is beyond belief," remarked one celebrant to an Al-Jazeera news reporter. "I mean, who could have imagined?"

The man smiled, blending into the sea of J.P. supporters as he disappeared. Meanwhile, celebrations unfolded nationwide, including in Wilmington, Delaware, where Jean Pierre was scheduled to deliver a speech in the evening. Atlanta, Seattle, and Minneapolis also experienced eruptions of joy. In Chicago, a video captured an individual cheering and banging a pot while a child broke into a spontaneous dance with a tambourine. In Miami, diners at various establishments could be seen clapping and cheering as news of Jean Pierre's triumph was announced."

"I am excited," celebrant Craven Hooks told NBC Philadelphia. "I am hoping this will be a new era."

In the crowd in Washington, D.C., was twenty-four-year-old Georgia Solomon, a clinical lab associate who said the election of Senator Bilac as vice president would inspire minorities to continue striving.

"I think Jean Pierre and Bilac symbolize more hope for us as a race and as women to empower ourselves to do better and to know that we can make an impactful change to America," she said.

Brianna Nappi, a thirty-five-year-old Italian who worked for the city, said, "Jean Pierre's ascension means we made it."

"We've seen, and we're free," she said. "That's how I feel."

****

The U.S. Presidential Election takes place every four years on the first Tuesday in November. Traditionally, candidates publicly declare their intention to run for president in the year before the election. Since no national authority conducted the elections, local authorities organized the election with the help of thousands of administrators.

Due to technical leverage and years of almost clandestine campaigning, Senator Jerry Bilac was elected by an electoral college consisting of members of both Houses of Parliament under the system of proportional representation employing the single transferable vote, and the voting in such election was by secret ballot. The Electoral College elected a person to the office of the Vice-President consisting of all members of both Houses of Parliament.

In other U.S. elections, candidates were elected directly by popular vote. However, the President and vice president were not elected directly by citizens. Instead, they were chosen by "electors" through the Electoral College. The process of using electors came from the Constitution.

Now, Gilbert Mathews, the Republican of German descent, Ted Dumby, and many others from Team Jean Pierre and Jerry Bilac were part of the team of "electors." The Vice President was elected along with the President by the Electoral College. Each elector cast one vote for President and another for Vice President.

The presidential election of 2024 revealed a need to amend the U.S. Constitution. The original system for electing presidents provided that the candidate receiving the most Electoral College votes would become President while the runner-up would become vice president.

The 2024 election had initially resulted in a tie between Joe Biden and Jean Pierre. Under the Constitution, this stalemate sent the election to the House of Representatives, which chose Jean Pierre. The states soon ratified a twelfth amendment to the Constitution, requiring separate contests for the President's and vice president's offices.

To establish a balance in resolving tied vice-presidential contests, the Twelfth Amendment mandated that the Senate assume responsibility. The Senate was tasked with selecting one candidate from the top two recipients of electoral votes, requiring a two-thirds majority of Senate members for a decision.

Although the Hawks employed specific underhanded tactics, they were careful not to overstep their boundaries. They engaged in covert "whisper campaigns," spreading rumors, innuendos, and slanderous remarks discreetly, tarnishing reputations and undermining financial support and backing. The targets of these campaigns were Joe Biden and Kamala Harris.

However, the candidates were caught in a Catch-22 situation: publicly denouncing the rumors would only draw more attention to the issue, while ignoring the clandestine whispers risked damage to their campaigns. With the assistance of speechwriter Gloria Winston, presidential candidates Ronald McBride, Jeff Bradyon, and Walter Newton-Smith willingly withdrew their candidacies under Jerry Bilac's influence. Instead, they joined forces to elevate the French gentleman to the highest position of power, successfully advancing their collective agenda.

Jerry Bilac and Dumby had simultaneously been working on the Vice Presidency of Bilac for almost a year now. They had been extremely reticent about the escapade, letting only a few 'close' associates know. The Hawks had also resorted to 'Push polling,' an unfair and unethical political device to communicate negative messages.

Under the guise of conducting a legitimate poll, defamatory or otherwise damaging information is usually conveyed, and false information is generally transmitted. The main target of this was ex-Vice President Kamala Harris. Her headscarf, faith, and hijab were demonized to the extent of reducing her to tears as she stepped down.

For Jean Pierre, the Republicans had employed and

eventually benefited from unfair competition. Unethical practices aimed at impeding fair competition for opponents were prevalent. It was common for affluent candidates to hire numerous political consultants, not primarily for their expertise, but to prevent them from working with their opponents. In their pursuit of victory, the Hawks resorted to this tactic, strategically purchasing the services of political consultants from all directions for the past year, ensuring that their actions remained undetected.

****

Jean Pierre and Sylvie were ecstatic. They joyfully said, "We finally made it."

"Indeed, we did, J.P." Bilac's smile had changed since the evening of the elections.

"Now we're opening many, many more restaurants in America and changing how America eats," Sylvie said, resting her head on her husband's shoulder.

"In Good Food, we trust," added J.P.

"We are going change the way America eats and much more." Jean Pierre played the traditional role of Europe's "Old Soul," even though he was barely in his fifties. The couple looked perfect with their good looks and taste in fashion, designer clothes with J.P. raised a few feet from the ground, seemingly lost in a haze of literary romanticism and a deep sense of history, lingering in the air, right above his head.

He channeled a more nonchalant, "je ne sais quoi - I do not know what."

The couple looked like Vogue, Gentlemen's Quarterly, Vanity Fair, Madame Figaro, Tétu, and other high-fashion magazines today. Many Parisian men have moved beyond the beret and pencil-thin moustache and unshaved beard stereotype, but some timeless classics remain.

Jean Pierre's supporters strategically used the "October surprise"—a last-minute hostile attack before an election to catch the target off guard and reduce their chances of responding—to rally behind him. This tactic involved presenting assertions in a way that delayed a response, often disadvantaging the targeted party.

Mobile phones rang amid the celebration, sending messages of anticipation from world leaders eager to work with Jean Pierre Labaguette (correct spelling) on Wednesday, January 20th, when he becomes U.S. president. This ended four years of Democratic rule. As expected, the French President was the first to contact President Labaguette, demonstrating their strong relationship.

"Félicitations à Jean Pierre," his voice rang out of the ear piece of the Panasonic cordless landline. "Il est temps de ramener la conviction et le bon sens et de rajeunir notre relation UE-États-Unis."

"Congratulations, J.P. It's time to bring back conviction & common sense and rejuvenate our EU-US relationship."

"Bon jour, السلام عليكم"

Peace be upon you.

" .أفهم أنك قضيت ليلة طويلة le président,"

"I understand you had a long night."

"Who is there?"

"أخوك من فرنسا علي بن سعود"

"Your brother, from France, Ali Bin Saoud"

"Je vais vous dire quelque chose de bien."

"I'll tell you something, though."

"ضربت عصفورين بحجر واحد".

"Kill two birds with one stone."

"Battre le fer pendant qu'il est Chaud."

"Strike while the iron is hot."

"Je ne veux pas – Je ne comprends pas ton arabe.

"I won't. I do not understand your Arabic."

"حبيبي, maintenant que vous êtes l'homme le plus puissant au monde, vous et moi devons parler à Jean Pierre, M. le Président.

"My love, now that you're the most powerful man on earth, you and I need to talk, Jean Pierre, Mr. President."

"Bien. Laisse-moi me calmer, on peut parler.

"OK. Let me calm down, we can talk."

"Fine حبيبي, que vous le souhaitez. مع السلامة"

"As you like. Bye."

Jean Pierre quickly put the phone on a table nearby and walked back to the group. Bilac, Sylvie, Dumby, and now they were joined by Jeremy Richards, who was pushing inside a trolley with a wine bucket and a bottle of 1811 Chateau d'Yquem. The trolley also had other beverages.

"Here you go, Mr. Dumby."

"Chateau d'Yquem?" Bilac almost shouted, "What the fuck for?"

"Calm down, man. These are happy times."

"And broke times. Dumby, you do not want to open that $200,000 wine bottle."

"Quoi? 200,000 $?"

"What, $200,000?"

J.P. looked at Dumby. "I want to unopen the bottle. Ask your servant to get the corkscrew."

"Hey, hey, hey... Jeremy is not my servant or anyone else's."

"Alors? Ton père?"

"Then? Your father?"

"Enough with the French."

"Ferme ta grande gueule, idiot."[36]

"He gestured for Jeremy to bring the bottle to him. "I am President now. I can do anything, drink, eat, say anything, tu comprend?"

"Did you call me an idiot?" Bilac tried to get near Jean Pierre, but Dumby stepped between them.

"Quit it, guys. You two are the most powerful men on this planet, for fuck's sake, and bickering like children?

Jean Pierre was getting messages of congratulations. Some of the world leaders called were 'schemers' and 'adventuresses,'

---

[36] "Shut your big mouth, you idiot."

and what they were doing, the papers crowed, was nothing short of a racket.

When the French President had called, the legislation in question was the "breach of promise" or "heart balm" suit, and it was based on the premise that an engagement was a binding contract between two people. He had never thought that he would ever receive a call from him.

However, the regulation automatically transferred itself to him when Jean Pierre did. It was under the shadow of this measure of codification that J.P. had to be mindful, especially when speaking to leaders with an agenda. "Merci Mr. Présidente."

He started sweating in an otherwise cold room, "J'ai hâte de vous voir bientôt."[37]

Next was the Prime Minister of England, Mr. John Patel, a short man of about five-two, with a wheatish skin tone and a squeaky voice as if speaking from his ass. Patel was half Indian, half Bengali. Mr. Patel was not an Indian citizen, and a parent or grandparent of his, he was born in British India before 1948 when India was part of the British Empire. He was born and bred in Liverpool, grew up to become a politician, and finally came to power in September of 2022 when he became Prime Minister, forcing his predecessor to step down.

"Hello," Mr. Patel spoke the received pronunciation, an accent mixed between Liverpool and New Delhi. "President Jean Pierre?"

"Yes, I am talking."

---

[37] "I look forward to seeing you soon."

"Cheers, mate, I'm chuffed to bits at the news. This is fit." He paused, "You're not really, er...."

"What?"

"Nothing, even though I'm knackered. I just returned from Portugal, but calling and chatting with you is extremely important. Did I mention you look smart? You and the missus."

"The First Woman, you mean," J.P. responded.

"Er, the first lady, that's correct." Then, after a beat, "She's very lush."

"M'excuser!

"Excuse me!"

What you said?"

"She's quite tidy, isn't she? "And you look smashing tonight. Where is the Houndstooth blazer from?"

"Yves Saint Laurent. How's Mrs Patel?"

"Hunky-dory. She's a picnic short of a sandwich," He snickered.

"OK, Mr. Patel, I need you to let me go."

"Mate, nobody has your posh behind in chains."

"What you say?"

"I said, sure, go ahead, nuke some poor, starving, flooded countries." Prime Minister Patel laughed this time. "You can start with Pakistan."

"What are you even telling me?"

"Just don't get your knickers in a twist."

"I am not understanding."

"Poppycock!" PM Patel's voice sounded like he had moved away from the phone, "You're still gobsmacked. I'll ring you later, Jean Pi... Mr. President."

"OK."

"Ta-ta!"

"You too," J.P. pushed the cordless end-call button.

He looked at Bilac, who was looking at him inquisitively. "You good chief?"

"I need a drink...." The phone rang again.

Before Dumby could tell him not to answer the phone and let the operator do it, Jean Pierre had pressed the 'OK' button on the Panasonic. "Hello?"

"Namaste jee, ees thees Babbaeshwari, New Delhi Biryani Carner?"

"Bien sûr que non!

"Hell no."

How do you connect, how do you connect?" Jean Pierre shouted into the phone before slamming it down on its cradle.

The phone rang again as soon as J.P. hung up.

"Don't answer Jean... Mr. President."

J.P. didn't pay any attention, "Hello."

"Mr. President, this is the Secret Service. We would appreciate it if you would not respond to calls directly before they're screened."

"Who are you?"

"The Secret Service, I'm Col. (Ret.) Karl Bourbon. Nice to make your acquaintance, Mr. President. We have heard a lot...."

"Yes, yes..." Jean Pierre interrupted the retired colonel, "Listen, Karl Urban."

"Bourbon."

"Whatever the frying fish ever! I will answer any calls I want to, you or nobody."

There was silence on the other end. Jean Pierre hung up. The phone rang again. This time, Dumby answered.

"It's for you," He gave the handset to Jean Pierre. J.P. looked at Bilac from the top of his eyes and then back to the phone.

"Zut, alors! Oui, Hello."

"These eez Dinreç Ebu Bekir from Germany. Jean P... I mean, Mr. President?"

"Yeah."

"Sesinizi duymak ne kadar hoş

"How nice to hear your voice"

"Ce qui?

"What?"

"Herzlichen Glückwunsch.

"Congratulations."

Jean Pierre looked irked, "Listen, whoever you are, I can't understand a word you're saying, so goodbye...."

"Ben Almanya'dan Ebu Bekir, Tebrikler Jean Pierre

"I'm Ebu Bekir from Germany, Congratulations Jean

101

Pierre."

" Jean Pierre had pressed end call on the handset and blue-penciled the long-distance call, just like that.

"Who was it?" Bilac asked.

"Some funny man talking in some funny way; I think it was a crank call from German."

"Germany? Prank call. No, it wasn't. This is the White House, Jean Pierre. We don't get prank calls here."

J.P. ignored Bilac. "Where are the wines?"

"Did you hear what I just said?" Bilac raised his voice.

"Comment osez-Vous?

"How dare you?"

"Sylvie raised her voice, "he is the President of the United States. You will be done as he speaks."

Bilac looked at Dumby, who returned his bewildered gaze.

"What the hell just happened to the French clown? He went from humble to Nimrod in ten!?" Dumby thought.

"Mr. President," Margarette Cobblepot held a phone in her hand as she called on him.

"Yes, honey?" Jean Pierre smiled.

"What you mean 'honey'? She your 'honey,' go sleep on her, go. Tu es un Cochon misogyne

"You're a misogynistic pig."

" Sylvie worked up.

Margarette stepped back after handing the phone to

Dumby.

"L'habit ne fait pas le moine."

"The outfit doesn't make the monk."

"Jean Pierre dismissed Sylvie. "Je déteste parler à la tête de couches

"I hate talking to diaper heads."

"Putain, je déteste les terroristes musulmans."

""Fuck. I hate Muslim terrorists. They now become world leaders.

"Que Dieu protège la France."

"God save France."

"I believe it's for you." Dumby extended the cordless towards Jean Pierre, who still had his eyes fixed on his wife and snatched the phone from Dumby. "Yes? Make it hurry up."

****

The Republicans' most important move was to stay the course, keeping out of Biden's way as old age crept in and Biden could be seen shaking hands with imaginary people. "He's losing his mind, and soon he will be gone, if not dead, then perhaps dementia will set in, and that's it for that presidency."

"It's always been my feeling that Biden would defeat Biden." Dumby said, "Part of politics is being good, and part of politics is being lucky, and J.P. is fortunate to have that Scranton handshake as an opponent.

"Plus." Dumby continued, "He'd had his chance to run in

2016, the conventional wisdom went, and now the party seems to be seeking something else – a firebrand to reinvent it."

"With eight years of that French Cook in the White House, the very essence and identity of our nation will be irrevocably transformed," Bilac expressed with concern. "I cannot simply stand idly by and witness such a profound change unfold."

Dumby calmly poured himself a glass of water from the dispenser and walked peacefully."

Sometime later!

Dumby and Vice President Bilac were sitting in the Cabinet Room, a bright, glass-walled meeting room for the officials and advisors to the President of the United States who constitute the Cabinet of the country. The room was located in the West Wing of the White House, adjoining the Oval Office, and looked out upon the White House Rose Garden.

Dumby had his gaze fixed on the dream-like Victorian garden under glass. The inspiration for renewing the rose garden at the White House came from President Kennedy in 1961. Hardly had the President and Mrs. Kennedy come ashore from his boat when he suggested discussing a garden for the White House while on a picnic on a hazy summer day in August at a beach house on Cape Cod, surrounded by dunes, the sea, and sailboats.

He and Mrs. Kennedy had just returned from a state visit to France, followed by stops in England and Austria. The President noted that the White House had no garden that was equal in quality or attractiveness to the gardens he had seen and in which he had been entertained in Europe. There, he recognized the importance of gardens surrounding an official residence and their appeal to the sensibilities of all people.

Eager to commence immediately, he strongly desired to renovate the vicinity adjacent to his office, the Rose Garden, located at the west end of the White House. His vision was to transform it into a practical and visually appealing space.

Accompanying VP Bilac and Dumby were J.C. Long, the chief usher, and Derek Wheeler, a Washington-based landscape architect who had been summoned by Jean Pierre a week earlier after obtaining his contact information from Maggie, the GOP Business Card. Jean Pierre informed Wheeler and Long that he intended to implement a "few" alterations to the structure.

They introduced themselves to Wheeler, and upon knowing that he was an architect, both Dumby and Bilac shifted in their chairs. "What? When?"

"What do you mean, Mr. Vice President?" Wheeler asked, leaning in.

"No, nothing, I was only wondering... Did Jean Pierre call you?"

"You mean the President?"

"Yes, the President of the United States, Jean Pierre Labaguette."

"Nope."

"Huh?"

"His pretty wife did."

"Sylvie?" Bilac said with eyes wide open.

Wheeler nodded, and Long just sat there, listening to their conversation.

"What'd she say?" Dumby asked.

"I'm afraid I can't tell you."

"What do you mean? I'm the vice president," Bilac raised his voice.

"Yes, but you're not the president now?"

Bilac sighed, got up, and left. Dumby excused himself and followed Bilac. "Hey, wait up."

Bilac stalled and put his hands into his trousers' pockets. "We've created a monster!"

"Nah, don't say that. It's not that bad."

"Dumby, it's the first day of his presidency. First, he wants the incumbent president out before the twenty-one-day protocol, and he wants to swap the menu for his fancy French food. Now, he's bloody outsourcing the 'restructuring' of the White House to an unknown architect. Can you believe that? He wants to reorganize the architect of the White House."

"Hmmm. All right, let me speak with him."

Bilac looked at him and frowned, "What will you tell him? Don't mess with the heritage?"

"No. I have something in mind. If it works, we will have that French clown under our thumbs; we still do, just that he doesn't know, similar to Trump being in denial when he lost to that old timer."

"Denial or power-hungry?"

"Same thing," Dumby paused for a moment. "Listen, the Republicans are back with a vengeance, and I can see it in the eyes of the freaking doves, scared like wet kittens."

"Who wouldn't be when we have a Kim Jong-un in the making."

"You're being Paranoid, Senator. I mean Vice Presi...."

"Just call me Bilac."

Dumby glinted, "We can pass our agenda easily."

Bilac looked at Dumby.

"It doesn't matter if he becomes a God. We control that French cook; all we need is time for him and his wife to truly understand how things work here, and then we're in business."

"What happens before that?"

"We wait and play his game."

9

The Speech

"Aggression unopposed becomes a contagious disease."

— Jimmy Carter

An ultra-luxurious €30,000 L. Leroy Marine Chronographe Automatique stainless steel and alligator strap watch ornamented Jean Pierre's right wrist. He wore that exorbitant timepiece.

He curated a stylish ensemble effortlessly by skillfully combining a Maison Kitsuné off-white linen, wool, and silk-blend blazer with a Tom Ford periwinkle blue slim-fit suede western overshirt. This was complemented by slim-fit washed cotton-blend trousers from Polo Ralph Lauren, which sat at the perfect height to showcase the Christian Louboutin Samson Studded Leather Chelsea Boots.

He had spent time with his French Tailor in New York, Mister Aloïs Mylan, at his store, Mylan Custom Tailors, at 1386 2nd Ave, New York.

Sylvie opted for a slightly larger than her frame COS Oversized Fit Checked Blazer in beige that could've been from a menswear closet, from her husband's, for all we know. She had added an Isabel Marant Lecce leather waist belt over the blazer for a more feminine look.

Under the blazer, she wore a bright white Zadig & Voltaire Linen Relaxed Shirt. Her Loulou Studio black wide-leg pants covered her Gucci Ace water snake-trimmed embroidered leather sneakers. French women wear sneakers quite frequently, even in the streets of Paris. Sneakers or trainers are an essential shoe style found in every French woman's closet.

"Hardly any French woman chooses high heels for the whole day. Instead, in Paris, it's far more common to see women wearing comfortable flat shoes such as ballet flats, loafers, and sneakers. In terms of her wristwatch, she exuded humility by adorning a modest yet elegant Omega Aqua Terra 150M with a silver chain bracelet. Alongside this, she sported Burberry sunglasses, radiating a captivating aura, much like her husband.

The sight of the elegantly attired French couple stirred a sense of admiration among the Americans, who instinctively associated them with qualities of quality, craftsmanship, and exquisite design. Yet, despite their appreciation, discerning the precise elements that distinguished the most fashionable French individuals proved elusive to the citizens of the United States. In their eyes, the allure of French style remained a captivating enigma, characterized by an elusive elegance that transcended mere fashion trends. Each glance at the impeccably dressed couple served as a poignant reminder of the enduring mystique surrounding French fashion, leaving observers mesmerized by its timeless charm and effortless sophistication.

They thought to themselves as they cheered on the eye candy of a couple, now a power couple, the President and First Lady of the most powerful country in the world and the first two levels of heaven. Most of the onlookers had gathered at the Ellipse, situated south of the White House fence and north of Constitution Avenue and the National Mall in Washington, DC. The anticipation was high for the new President's Endorsement Speech.

The attendees wore neutral-colored clothing, characterized by relaxed and comfortably tailored garments with impeccably fitted shoulders. Notably, the President opted for a collar that popped distinctly, eschewing a tie and adding a sense of individuality to his ensemble. The jacket's fit suggests the suit may be bespoke.

However, not everyone was ecstatic, not even close to happy. The French-born and raised man's ascension to the Presidency left them profoundly disturbed and angry. As the Congress geared up to validate the win of Biden's replacement, President Labaguette vehemently criticized the Democrats and their failed policies during the Biden era.

Vice President Jerry Bilac encouraged this, leading to events that eventually sparked hours of violence as ordinary people clashed on the streets. The Republicans and the Democrats were also breathing down each other's necks and, in this case, also down their necks.

Shortly before leaving the White House, in a Peugeot with two French buses following JP and his men on Wednesday morning for the Ellipse, where a podium with the American Symbol had been set up for President Labaguette to address supporters. The Chief of Staff had a word with Mr. Bilac.

A day prior, Mr. Bilac reiterated his earlier conversation with Mr. Labaguette. He made it clear that when he headed to Capitol Hill in a few hours to supervise the electoral vote count, officially confirming J. P. Labaguette's triumph, he lacked the authority to fulfill the President's desire to overturn the outcome. Mr. Bilac intended to issue a letter shortly detailing his decision and explaining it.

The chief of staff listened, stewed, and chastised Mr. Bilac as soft. He accused Mr. Bilac's right-hand man, Ted Dumby. He was responsible for Mr. Bilac's position and told his aides that Mr. Dumby was working at the White House complex before the joint session of Congress began. He was "not welcome" there.

Once Mr. President was on the podium set for him at the Ellipse, he initiated the Endorsement Speech, authored by the Republican speech writer Gloria Winston."

"I am honored by your nomination, and I accept it with pride, gratitude, and a total will to win a great victory for the American people. I will wage a winning campaign in every region of this country, from the snowy banks of Minnesota to the sandy plains of Georgia. I concede not a single State. I concede not a single vote."

"The speech says 'we.' Why did he say 'I'?" Gloria wondered.

President Jean Pierre Labaguette continued, trying to explain to the layman the innovative measures that his Presidency would take, "This evening I am proud to stand before this great convention as the first incumbent President since Dwight D. Eisenhower who can tell the American people America is at peace."

A virtual reality image of George Washington appeared next to JP on the podium. Bilac and Dumby looked at each other. "That can't be Gloria. We never mentioned anything about incumbency, and goddam Eisenhower, what the fuck is he talking about?"

Bilac was furious and added, "What is that virtual reality gimmick we paid a fortune on in his restaurant?"

"I'm sure he made her add that when he was rehearsing last evening," Dumby added.

Bilac turned his head towards the speaker, tilted his head a little, and crossed his arms. His two-tone Rolex shone in the November sun. Dumby did the same.

Mr. Jean Pierre Labaguette continued, "Tonight. I can tell you straightaway this Nation is sound, this Nation is secure, and this Nation is on the march to full economic recovery and a better quality of life for all Americans."

"And I will tell you one more thing. This year, the issues are on our side. I am ready. I am eager to go before the American people and discuss the real issues with the Russian Head of State, the Chinese Premier. The American people have a right to know firsthand where I stand."

"Again?" Gloria was getting worried, but deep down, she

knew what an egocentric piece of shit this JP guy was.

"I am deeply grateful to those who stood with me in winning the restaurant nomination. I mean the party whose cause I have served all my adult life. I respect the convictions of those who want a change in the various delicacies being served throughout the great country, mainly in Washington. I want a change, too."

This was when two people got into a physical altercation in Utah Valley while the speech was being broadcast on the newly installed giant movie screen in Utah County. The 3D Mammoth Screen at Thanksgiving Point, sixty-three feet wide by forty-five feet tall, is now in the mainstream movie business.

The fight broke out at the 3D Mammoth Screen at Thanksgiving Point in Lehi. This was the first of many conflicts that were to take place during the day and go on until evening, when Riot Control Police would be called in with their batons, rubber bullets, and fiberglass shields.

"Your fucking president is only interested in food."

"They just want to look flashy. Just look at them. Their clothes must be worth at least half a mil."

"Is the First Lady wearing a pair of Adidas? What nonsense!"

"Give him six months, and we will become extinct."

"Six months? The Europeans already have a ball, not to mention the fucking Israelis."

"Oh goodness, what next, a Muslim Judge at the Supreme Court?"

This backlash was not limited to the Utah Valley. The supporters of JP Labaguette and his detractors were at odds with each other. The fissure was as wide as the White House swimming pool. The crack kept widening to Alaska from New York to Los Angeles, Chicago to Houston, Phoenix to Philadelphia, San Antonio to San Diego, and Mississippi to Truth or Consequences.

"We tried Trump. What good did he do?"

"Biden is half in his grave. We need someone new, and young and...."

"Someone with limited knowledge of The Americas."

"They both look so good together."

"I'm sure we are heading for a huge, positive change."

****

President Labaguette continued, laying down his agenda one after the other, starting with a measure against divorce. "It takes effort to protect, nurture, and grow a marriage. Between work schedules, children, and other obligations, sometimes it can seem impossible to maintain that partnership. When problems arise, some couples find it healthier to divorce and separate. For others, it's a better choice to work on the relationship. If you want to stay with your partner and avoid divorce, there are proactive measures you can take. From improving communication to infusing more romance into day-to-day life."

"Is he serious?" Dumby asked, shocked at what he had just heard. He took out his phone and started to dial Gloria.

Bilac had one hand on his face. He lowered his hand and turned towards Dumby, "Who are you calling?"

"Gloria."

"Not now, Dumby, not now. Wait for a little."

Dumby shut his phone and put it back with a frown on his face.

The President continued, "... Even if you never voice those thoughts. The thought alone might cause a major break in your motivation to improve your marriage." He stopped abruptly and looked around. He gestured for someone to come close to him. The secret agent men all got alerted and started to advance towards Mr. Labaguette. "It okay, it fine – I'm calling it to read what I can't."

Carter Evans, the photographer standing near the podium, came running and was immediately blocked by the men in black until JP put his hand on one of their shoulders and asked them to let him through. "We can't do that, Mr. President, not during the speech," one of the secret agent men said in a whisper.

"I told you, let him enter."

They did, and as soon as Evans was at his side, JP pointed to a word in his notes. Carter whispered it to him. JP smiled and started again, "Where were we?"

"He can't even speak English without looking at his notes. What an idiot."

"Ah, yes." Mr. President said, "People inevitably change over time. Understanding, appreciating, and adapting to those changes is critical for any relationship. Start by listing your partner's best qualities to remind yourself of the wonderful person you married."

He smiled at his wife.

"Whatever your situation is when you blurt out 'divorce,' it is strongly advised that you mean it rather than issuing an empty threat to blow off steam. The idea of divorce is the ultimate abandonment and goes to the core of people's attachment issues. So, even though it is only at the moment and not meant, the threat has been put out there and is frightening, says psychologist and author Dr. Karen Sherman."

"Finally, someone who favors family units and not binaries."

"I told you, this guy has it in him to tackle the most sensitive matters."

"I love our new President; his wife is so damn pretty."

He paused, looked back, and tried to find Gloria, who could not be seen.

"What has she written? I can't even have pronounced words like these," He thought, and then JP decided to jump to the next topic.

"Marriage will have to be renewed yearly after a financial analysis and psychological interview, and that yearly renewal will give a tax credit."

"Divorce insurance will be mandatory."

Dumby started to shake. "We will lose the support of all the divorce lawyers. This is a catastrophe."

"Taxes. I will diminish income taxes but generate income from a new tax on selfies. Selfies are a narcissistic, unproductive past time which is dangerous in many ways."

Dumby felt dizzy, "We have lost all our young voters."

"We will implement a program of artificial intelligence to

monitor the corruption of Congress, conflict of interest, money transfer, and fiscal paradise interest."

"We have lost the support of Congress!"

"After four long years of majority misrule, let's change the United States Congress," JP said. "Improved race and ethnicity measures reveal US population is much more multiracial."

"Huh? Did he say that?" CEO Samuel Peterson said as he watched JP on the same Sony LCD, they had learned of his contention at 671 Seneca St. Buffalo, in the office building of the Erie County Democratic Committee.

"Yes, you heard him," James Bullard said, not shifting his glance from the TV.

"He just handed us the lawyers' support and the narcissists."

Back at the Ellipse, the new President-elect continues, "These changes reveal that the US population is much more multiracial and diverse than we measured in the past.

"I am confident that differences in the overall racial distributions are mainly due to improvements in the design of the two separate questions for race data collection and processing as well as some demographic changes over the past ten years.

"I am also confident, as shown in our research, that using a single combined question for race and ethnicity in the decennial census would yield an even more accurate portrait of how the US population self-identifies, especially for people who self-identify as multiracial or multiethnic. Slowly but surely, riots are breaking out in small groups nationwide. People are bickering at their workplaces, also. People watching the speech on their handheld devices are also divided, like how all of America is."

"Isn't this good?"

"What is so good about a French chef taking over our country?" shouted an onlooker

"Save the Burgers and Hot Dogs." replied his lady friend.

"Don't forget you're also a refugee."

"What do you mean by 'also'; this ass isn't a refugee, and I'm not even running for the Branch Manager position at Macy's."

****

President Jean Pierre Labaguette continued, "My gratitude Tonight reaches far beyond this arena to countless friends whose confidence, hard work, and unselfish support have brought me to this moment. It would be unfair to single out anyone, but may I make an exception for my wonderful family in France, especially my dear wife, Sylvie, and my children, Patrick and Jacqueline."

"What? Not a single mention of...."

"Be patient, Dumby. Wait, this guy is not as stupid as we thought."

President Labaguette kept listing points from his 'innovative measures' agenda, "I will implement the import exemption for French food imports. There shall be a change of Police Uniforms to softer colors, light blue for the males and pink for the female officers."

"We just lost the support of the police," whispered Dumby

"All right, that's it. Pull the damn plug," Dumby tried to get up from his chair. Bilac held him by his left arm and pulled him back, and Ted slumped back.

"Not now, Dumby."

"But, Bilac, Mr. Vice President..."

"Bilac, call me Bilac."

"Yeah, okay. Bilac, if we don't stop this now, God knows what he will say next."

"You want to stop him in the middle of the Endorsement? They'll put you behind bars, Ted. Now keep sitting and let this end."

"The speech or the country?"

****

"As a Republican, I have had some tough competition. I do not only preach the virtues of competition. I practice those. But tonight, we come together not on a battlefield to conclude a cease-fire but to join forces on a training field that has conditioned us all for the rugged contest ahead. Let me say this from the bottom of my heart: After the scrimmages of the past few months, it feels good to have Mr. Trump on the same side of the line."

The team of Republicans started panicking. They blamed each other and contested JP's birth certificate.

"Are you sure he was born in the USA?" Ronald asked Dumby.

"Isn't it a little too late for that to investigate the birth records? He showed them to us. Remember when he said he was born in South Carolina? Cooking and food are like politics?"

"I wasn't there," Ronald Despots responded.

"Well, that sounds like what a beer-colored glass would say now, in real life, doesn't it?"

Jefferson Groundplain said.

"Look what Minority Report says after what he did in 2020. Beer colored? Jeff, man, you're trippin' on your Skittles. What the heck were you thinking when you picked that black fifteen-year-old? "Walter Matthews spoke up.

"I didn't know."

"Just like how we don't, right now. Bloody pedo kitty."

"Shut up, just shut up, Mr. Matthews, before I smack you."

"I'd like to see you try."

10

The Speech (Part 2)

"The art of war is simple enough. Find out where your enemy is.
Get at him as soon as you can. Strike him as hard as you can,
and keep moving on."

— Ulysse S. Grant

Sylvie stood by her husband's side as he addressed the crowd and the people from the Press. She whispered something in his ear. He looked at her and nodded.

"What's that fashion bimbo saying to him, now?" Dumby wondered.

"I have no idea," Bilac responded.

"My most beautiful wife, Sylvie, has decided to remodel the white house with the help of French fashion Designers. Maybe Cartier or Givenchy or Claudie Pierlot or Balmain, who will be hired personally by her".

"That interference is getting outta line."

"We crossed the sanity line when we first entered his stupid restaurant. What is it called? He's opened so many after that, I can't remember."

"Restaurant Jean Pierre Labaguette."

"Ah, yes, that one," Bilac rubbed his forehead. "Next, she'll want to dirty bomb Turkey, and JP will most happily turn the key and press the red button."

"It takes two..."

"I know. I'm the guy with the second key," Bilac informed Dumby. "But he thinks he'll be running our Nation alone. What a retard."

JP continued, "The convention had a wise choice, one of the ablest ever Americans as my forthcoming Vice President, Senator Jerry Bilac of Kansas. "With his little helper, with my big helping, with the second big helping of Sylvie who loves all of you ...." He stopped and bent to take a closer look at the word, "prosper-city shared, and probe, sorry, proud, no, no, prize in America, I have won this election. This isn't a Republican victory, but also a victory for Sylvie, me, and the French-American love affair."

"A man stepped up and whispered into JP's ears."

"Yeah, yes, and also victorious of the Americans?" He started to laugh. Some people in the crowd flinched, others laughed, and the Bald Eagle was on the verge of a mental breakdown.

President Labaguette continued with his cringe-inducing speech. Jean Pierre made deliberate and volatile changes in the script: "Permit to having children: I will make sure that before having a child, American couples must apply for permission, called a birth permit. In rural areas, couples may apply for a birth permit to have a second child if their firstborn is a girl, and couples are allowed a maximum of three children if they are of an ethnic minority.

He turned toward his children and smiled at them. "They will have to take classes in parenting, including how to raise a healthy child, how to deal with erratic children's behavior without drugging them with prescription medications, how to keep them away from drugs and guns, and most of all, how to cook like a French person."

"We just lost the Pharmaceutical industry support!!! This is crazy," whispered Dumby, and the "Gun manufacturers," replied Bilac.

"The statuses of all Illegal aliens, except those from Muslim countries, in Federal, State, and Local Criminal Justice Systems will be tried again without inspectorate through the Immigration and Naturalization Service. In that place, I will decide who will stay and return home."

Once again, the same person from the last time came forward and whispered in JP's ears.

"We will legalize illegal drugs, which will become highly taxed controlled drugs. I intend to engage in talks with Narcos to have them grow under government control of our own US-made Cocaine and our US-made Cannabis. Narco traffickers will share their trade secrets and manufacturing know-how, and they will benefit by granting them a patent. They will make less money but they will avoid being in jail or killed."

"And we will reduce the carbon footprint and revive our rural areas. This is a 32 billion business. We will not let private individuals benefit from it while we pay for the customs and DEA expenses. I want Cocaine made in the USA and the Best Cannabis made in the USA, and we may even consider exporting to Peru, Mexico, and Colombia. This is our time to make drugs affordable and regulated. We did it for alcohol."

One guy from CNN asked him, "What about the Mexican Border Wall?"

"The Mexican Texas walls, as you can see..." he pointed to the image being projected on the projector screen. "When we get out to see, film, and map every footing of U.S.-Mexico bordering walls. This map will show you videography of the entire border and all the fences. We have a document from the air and the ground. I will double that wall. What do you call it?"

"Fortify!" Someone from the audience shouted.

"I'm not deaf. Yes, forty-five the wall.

Mexican can sell Taco or Fajita, Indian, no Mexican or Chinese food will be subsidized except French Food. "My Republican predecessor is not Julius Caesar. Donald Trump has no understanding of construction" he added "The wall has no deep foundation to prevent the South to North tunnels. I will continue engaging in the East and West Subway built by the French; we have already started planning the project. The total length of the project is between 2500 and 3,145 kilometers."

"Seoul subway, servant of the Seoul Metropolitan Area, is the longest subway system in the world. The total length of the system extended as far as 940 kilometers. Now, we need less than four times that length. The Great Wall of China is 21,196.18 kilometers. They did it for 100 years without modern technology. We can build with technology, homeless people, and illegal immigrants in two months."

"It is costly, 100 million per mile, but we will generate money by allowing advertising billboards and immigration lawyers are already committing to it We will cut down the cost of air transportation and carbon footprints of people and goods and interfere with drug smugglers' tunnels and coyote cartels. "I plan 45 subway stations along the border."

"We lost the Arline industry support," whipped Dumby.

"This is the Jean Pierre Pacific Atlantic subway line, as Jefferson or Obama said. I do not remember, "Yes, we can!" All 45 subway stations will be named after a US president."

"The Mexican-US border will no longer be a smuggler problem. It will be a hub of legal activities."

By now, the Hawks were ready to jump off any bridge.

"The 91st United States Congress, as Title II of the Comprehensive Drug Abuse Prevention and Control Act of 1971, signed by Nixon, will be amended to make Cocaine and meth legal but not for stores to open near schools and public parks. Prohibited, no, regulated, yes."

"Who does he think he is, Pablo Escobar, with a license?" Bilac said.

"No, The Rodríguez Orejuela couple, with Sylvie as Myriam Ramirez." Dumby went grim.

President Jean Pierre Labaguette described how he would bring about tremendous changes in the current policies, referring to Social Security, which he said he would reduce. He stated that French and not Spanish would be the second language. Further, he wanted to support the Canadian Separatists and move the army to the Canadian-US border if necessary. "The Nutritional Guideline will be based on French culinary recommendations."

The man came close to JP and corrected him again. The President went on forever.

"All Burgers Kings and Mac Burgers should sell as much baguette as burgers to keep their food license. We will also rename them McRoyale™. Today, French people will not require US Visas and will have reduced Airfare. We want to strengthen our relationships.

"Except for SUMO wrestlers, we will tax overweight travelers based on their Body Mass Index, they will have an overweight transport tax which can be exempted for medical reasons obviously."

"Negotiating will take place to sell Louisiana again to the French and Alaska to the Russians to reduce the debt with the Chinese, who are many." He spread his arms, "many!"

"You can't do that...." Someone shouted from the audience. JP looked behind him, and one of the men in a black suit approached the man, cuffed him, and took him away.

"Is there anything else I cannot do, my friendly people?"

An opposition member asked JP, "And what do you plan for climate change? The water levels are rising. Some coastlines will disappear within a few years?"

President JP smiled. "We have it in control, my friend. I have signed a contract with a French company for desalinization. We will take water off the ocean and take off the salt that we will use to make salt batteries as they are better and cheaper than lithium batteries. The water will be used for desert land. We will flood the Grand Canyon, which I will call 'Jean Pierre Lake Canyon.' And Las Vegas will be turned into a Dubai, with tallest buildings structures."

JP looked to his notes and continued, "The Grand Canyon has a volume of 7,345,724,462,194 Olympic-sized swimming pools."

The agent asked again, and JP was dismayed, "And what about the three million visitors?"

"They will become divers, snorkelers, fishermen, and boaters instead of wasting their time and money in the casinos."

"We have lost the Casino industry support," stuttered Dumby.

"Wait a minute. We are gaining the support of the outdoor and fishing industry. Not all is bad," answered Bilac. "JPL is a madman or a genius. We will look at the pool and act accordingly."

"What is your position on the LBGT? The gender issue?" asked the New York T.

"I believe that it comes from the food."

"What do you mean, Mr. President?"

"There are nearly 85,000 human-made chemicals worldwide, and 1,000 or more of those could be endocrine disruptors. Gender issues are prevalent in low-income, and we need to screen our population for endocrine disruptors in modern society."

"Vigilance is the key word here because there are so many chemicals," he opened his arms wide "so many" Understanding the effects of chemicals is a three-pronged approach. It's ensuring we have wildlife models and people watching wildlife populations to see quickly if something detrimental happens. It has outstanding epidemiological studies and shows the vigilance of people in various places. And it's backing those two up with laboratory science immediately when a problem arises to try to ascertain the cause quickly."

"He is a cook, a restaurateur a politician and an endocrinologist. That guy is dangerous," replied Bilac.

President JP Labaguette's ideas started some exciting debates within the population.

"He is mad."

"He is a genius."

"What is the difference between capitalism and socialism?"

Everyone looked around at each other.

JP suddenly answered without waiting, "In a capitalist society, man exploits man, and in a Socialist, it's the other way around." He started laughing hard, as did Sylvie, who laughed hard while everyone else was dumbfounded.

At the Republican's headquarters, the entire building echoed with the words, "We need to remove him!"

At the Democrats' headquarters, the building reverberated with the exact words, "We need to remove him!"

When the public thought the speech was over, JP started again, and a collective, audible moan traveled through the air. "You at home listening tonight. You are the people who pay the taxes and obey the laws. You are the people who make our system work. You are the people who make America what it is."

"Something terrible happened to our country in the past four years. We all came to realize it on the Fourth of July. Out of years of turmoil and tragedy, wars and riots, assassinations, viruses, and wrongdoing in high places, Americans recaptured the spirit of 1776. We again saw the pioneer vision of our revolutionary founders and immigrant ancestors. Their vision was of free men and women enjoying limited government and unlimited opportunity. "

"What an idiot!" All of America said that in unison.

"Having become President without expecting or seeking either and only opportunistic restaurant businesses, I have a special feeling toward these high offices. To me, the Presidency and the Vice Presidency were not prizes to be won but opportunities for restaurants to be opened all over The Americas, including Cuba."

"Cuba isn't America," whoever said that was escorted by a black suit to Gitmo, like the previous guy who had dared to oppose the French man.

JP smiled, "Not yet."

"So, tonight, it is not the power and the glamour of the Presidency that leads me to ask for four years; it is something every hard-working American will understand--the challenge of a job well begun but far from finished"

"Two nights past, I placed my hand on the Bible" he

whispered to his wife "with a copy of Vogue underneath," he smiled, "I did not have faith in our politicians and in most of our institutions, but only in myself."

"On that darkest day, I told my fellow countrymen, 'I am acutely aware that you have not elected me as your President by your ballots, so I ask you to confirm me as your President with your prayers and your choice of food, you are what you eat stop junk food."

Bilac abruptly halted his words, unable to locate Dumby in his usual spot. He softly called out Dumby's name but received no response. He dialed the number again and guessed he was busy with his regular high-end escort, Betty, at the Washington Hyatt, immersed in their intimate activities.

Bilac remarked, "It's better than having my mind tormented by a French lunatic." Then he ended the call."

JP was on the verge of concluding, but then he recollected and referred to his notes. "On a marble fireplace in the White House, there is an inscribed prayer that the John Adams family scrawled on walls. It prays, 'May none but honest and wise men ever rule under this roof.' As the most honest man in this jam-packed history, I have strived to live by that prayer. Even though I don't believe in God, we Trust, but in Food, we Trust."

"I have faced numerous daunting challenges. I haven't made any mistakes, but America and Americans have made an incredible resurgence since the pandemic."

"Nobody can honestly tell a lie. And the plain truth is that with great power comes great responsibility." JP paused for a moment. "Doesn't that line incredible? I just came up with it."

No one dared to question his assertion, and even those

watching from home fell silent as if a war had erupted between the US and the Hammer and Sickle.

Everyone could now discern which parts of the speech were scripted and when JP spoke off the cuff.

"My friends, Washington is not the problem; their Congress is the problem. The President of the United States is not a magician who can wave a wand or sign a document that instantaneously ends a war, resolves a recession, or eliminates bureaucracy. A President possesses immense powers under the Constitution, but ultimately, all stem from the American people and their mandate to the President."

He glanced at Gloria, shrugged his shoulders, and frowned. "No, only war, racism, and the troublemakers originate from the American people. The rest comes from me. That is why, tonight, all of you should turn to me and seek my prayers, strength, support, voice, and well-functioning digestive system."

"Fuck him. We need this guy to be out of that place. If he stays there for another week, we will go bankrupt, and the idiot will probably nuke the cities and states he doesn't like,'" Bullard said.

"The American people will not accept a double standard in the United States Congress. Those who make our laws today must not make the reputation of our great legislative hot body that has given us such giants as Daniel Webster, Henry Clay, Sam Rayburn, and Robert A. Taft ugly. Private morality and public Trust must go together in the Nation's Capital, the State capital, or city hall. But the best has just entered the game of thrones, me, Jean Pierre Labaguette!"

Sylvie moved a little closer to him and told him something.

"Yes, Sylvie will start renovation and making the Blue, White, and Red House. White is very boring. And Blue, White, and Red will look greatest."

"For the next four years, I pledge to hold the steady course we have begun. And I intend to stand alone," JP started to end his two-hour-long speech that had made America erupt in violence.

"As I try in my imagination to look into the homes where families are watching the end of this great convention, I can't tell which faces are Republicans, who are Democrats, and which are Independents. I cannot see their color or their creed. I see only Americans. Therefore, I will have cameras to be fixated in every home, building, office structure, and restaurant. That way, I will know who is who?"

"I see a new generation that knows what is right and knows itself. A generation determined to alter its ideals, its environment, and above all, change what the Nation stands for, and the world."

"I did not write that!" Gloria thinks to herself.

"My fellow Americans, I like what I see. I have no fear for the future of this great country. And as we go forward together, I promise you once more what I promised before to adjust the Constitution to become a healthy republic."

"It will be a great achievement for me"

Once again, Sylvie said something to him.

"And also, for America."

"I won't let you up. I mean down. One Nation, an indivisible nation, one artificial intelligence program under one

Supreme Leader, the great Jean Pierre Labaguette. Healthy Food for all and au revoir. Thank you very much."

****

"We have to undo this," whispered some republicans

"How?" Dumby asked.

"Damn, if I know, but this crazy fucker has to go."

"You got it, Dumby," Bilac said with eyes wide open. "But we need to keep it a secret."

11

The Sex Tape

"Any man worth his salt will stick up for what he believes right, but it takes a slightly better man to acknowledge instantly and without reservation that he is in error."

— Andrew Jackson

At the Republican Headquarters, Bilac, Dumby, James, and Glenn sat together.

"Remember JP twin brother?"

"Yup. What about him?"

"His twin brother is in jail because he killed one intruder. "

"Killed someone? A home invasion?"

"Yeah, in France, it is not allowed to kill an intruder.... " Dumby said casually.

"I mean, one of the two intruders killed his wife he killed one of them, and the other murderer is free pending psychiatric evaluation, " Dumby further explained.

****

"We have to get him out of jail and use him to start a scandal to overthrow our new President. "

"Rescue the brother, help him break out of the jail, fast and easy, "Bilac said.

"It will take a helicopter and some veteran mercenaries, "Walter added.

"We just have to find a day with a soccer match. The guards will be watching TV, "Dumby contributed. "Hmmm. "

"You got it, Dumby. "Bilac said with eyes wide open, "But we need to keep it a secret. "

****

The early sunrise painted a breathtaking scene, unlike anything nature had ever witnessed. The first light of dawn cast its radiant rays upon the horizon, creating an exquisite spectacle against the backdrop of billowing clouds. Shades of pink, gold, and orange adorned the heavens as if an artist's brush had delicately blended them. The gradual ascent of the sun transformed the sky into a resplendent canvas, where every corner became saturated with luminous sunlight.

Despite the weariness that clung to one's bones from rousing at such an early hour, the sight unfolding before their eyes made it all worthwhile. This moment marked the inception of a perfect day, promising endless possibilities and infinite wonders. Even the inmates, confined within their stark cells, found solace in the enchanting symphony of birdsong that permeated the air. Their melodic tunes drifted through the solitary iron-barred window carved into the distant recesses of Pierre Jean's cramped cell, granting him a fleeting connection to the outside world.

A chilly breeze danced through the wind, causing Pierre Jean to shiver. Yet, in his heart, he rejoiced. The scorching heat of the preceding summer weeks had finally relented, yielding to this refreshing zephyr. As the crisp gusts gently caressed his skin, they embraced the warmth that the sun bestowed upon his face, creating an ethereal harmony of sensations. It was a harmonious blend of the invigorating breeze and the tender touch of the sun's rays, rendering the moment even more spectacular as if nature itself had orchestrated this sublime symphony of elements.

"I cannot believe how little I have known about France before coming over here. I am ashamed to admit that France was for me associated only with Paris, Eiffel Tower, Romance, wine & cheese, croissants & baguettes, roasted chestnuts, snails, berets, and French men wearing scarves... so as you can see, my idea of France was from a perspective of an ignorant and I would like to apologize for this," the inmate who shared the cell with Pierre Jean said, in perfect English as they moved slowly, in a queue, towards the cemented yard as part of their morning routine. "The guards here are mostly hogs. "

Pierre Jean's gaze shifted towards the spoken voice, a gentle smile gracing his lips as he acknowledged the person's presence. With a momentary exchange of warmth, he returned his focus to the scene before him, captivated by the procession of heads stretching out in a seemingly endless line. Eager to catch a glimpse of what lay beyond, he strained to peer over the shoulder of the prisoner directly ahead, yearning for an enhanced view of the petite luminous opening that beckoned them towards the expanse of the sprawling courtyard. It looked like they were all waiting at the gates of heaven or some kind of hell.

Pierre Jean was of medium height and very similar to his brother. He had dark brown eyes and darker, curlier hair, and he was wearing a long-sleeved linen shirt, a denim jacket, and a pair of 1930s French tooling striped straight retro denim trousers. He had put on a light jacket today since it had become windy, and the cold had always hurt Pierre Jean's bones as soon as he crossed the thirty-five-year mark.

He wore regular clothes because prisoners in France did not wear uniforms and were instead provided with regular civilian clothing. The use of prison uniforms was abolished in 1983.

Pierre Jean the brother of Jean Pierre Labaguette, the new controversial President of the United States. He had watched his familiar face on the TV at many occasions, he couldn't quite comprehend his English, yet, however, the sharply dressed gent on the television was his blood. The notion had crossed his mind that the American President, accompanied by a lady named Sylvie, would undoubtedly stand out conspicuously amidst the sea of Caucasian and African American men, with their distinct

North American characteristics. They would either appear strikingly incongruous or shine like a rare and precious gem in this gathering. PJ had watched the President on the TV set in the Common area of a dorm area, as was the case with most French minimum-security prisons.

For years France has had the worst prison conditions in Western Europe. Prisons are old, more than half of them older than the Great War. They're overcrowded and filthy. Former President of France, President Nicolas Sarkozy, who served as President of France from 16 May 2007 until 15 May 2012, has called them a "national disgrace. "The European Court of Human Rights has condemned them several times.

Fleury-Mérogis is the largest prison in Europe, with some 4,000 inmates: men, women, and juveniles. Like Rikers in New York, it's meant to hold prisoners for just a year or so, including those on trial or awaiting sentencing. Long-term inmates have other facilities.

When it opened in 1969, Fleury-Mérogis was designed to house just 3,000. It was considered a modern solution to rundown, overcrowded jails of the postwar era, some of which were in ancient buildings. France was going through an earlier convulsion of guilt about prison reform.

Inmates screamed curses and catcalls from their barred windows as one group (the queue of prisoners) visited a small, empty sports yard ensconced between cell blocks. Plastic bags and punctured soccer balls were caught in the surrounding concertina wire.

"There were some radical Muslims who were putting huge pressure on regular Muslims to adopt a certain kind of behavior, like taking a shower with their clothes on and not listening to music or watching TV, "A young Arab inmate navigated between the fascist Islamic gang, the 'Illa-Naseeb' gang, and other not-so-crazy Arab gangs to rise to power in a vast, overcrowded prison. He spoke to himself as he worriedly walked towards Cell Block A, alone and not escorted by any prison guard, or an inmate. He was clad in a white robe, called a 'thoub,' 'dishdasha,' or 'kandora,' with a pair of loose-fitting trousers called 'sirwal.' He turned around the corner of Cell Block C and disappeared.

****

In the TV room

The gentleman next to PJ suddenly nudged PJ. "Oui? " PJ responded to the prodding.

"That's your relative, isn't it, JP? "The man said.

"Hein? Non? "JP said, annoyed a little, not because of what the man had said but because he felt the same: a relative or someone he knew very well a long time back.

"Je te dis que c'est ton frère."[38]

Delta Force, officially known as 1st Special Forces Operational Detachment-Delta (1st SFOD-D), was one of the U.S. special missions' units primarily focused on counterterrorism and rescue missions.

Though Delta Force is primarily a tier-one counterterrorism unit specifically directed to kill or capture high-value units or dismantle terrorist cells, Delta Force remains extremely flexible

---

[38] I'm telling you he's your brother

and can engage in direct-action missions, hostage rescues, and covert missions working directly with the CIA, as well as high-ranking protective services of our senior leaders

****

In Buffalo City, NY, Vice President Bilac and congressman Dumby were engrossed in a conversation in the same room where they had strategized Jean Pierre Labaguette's Presidential campaigning.

Dumby was the first to speak. He bent over to get closer to Bilac and spoke in a soft voice, "Compared to our military history, Delta is relatively young, having been formed in 1977 by its first commander, Col. Charles Beckwith. With the growing threat of terrorism around the world, Beckwith saw a need for a precision strike force within the Army after working with the British Special Air Service (SAS) in the early 1970s. "

"Where are you trying to go with all that? Why...? I mean, I don't need lessons in American Combat history. "

"History? Were you hiding under a rock for the past twenty-five years? "

"Get to the point, Dumby. I don't have all day."

"Well, guess what, Mr. Vice President, neither do I."

Bilac looked at Dumby with searing eyes that would penetrate his flesh.

"What? "Dumby asked when he saw the expression change on Bilac's face.

"Nothing. Go on."

"We have contacted Commander Lance Forsyth and tasked him to form the new unit and to pull his men largely from the Special Forces Groups. "He paused. "This is more than just a 'classified mission,' a clandestine operation. We will be entering the French airspace and breaking a whole lot of international peace treaty resolutions.... "

"Who gives a fuck? "Bilac retorted.

"Yeah, who gives a fuck? We're Americans. We can bloody well fly into and out of any country we want, whether they like it or not. "

"Correct. You were saying... And Dumby..."

"Yeah?"

"This better be worth my time, our time."

"Don't you worry, Mr. Vice President..."

"Do you remember Operation Eagle Claw?" Bilac did not look at Dumby as he asked him.

"Er. I have heard of...."

He didn't let Dumby finish. "During the Iran hostage crisis in 1980, a rescue attempt failed because of an aviation equipment/operator error and led to the deaths of eight Americans. As a result, the 160th Special Operations Aviation Regiment was created. "

"And? " Dumby was being just that, dumb.

"Mission, what have you... Have you given a name to the operation? "Bilac broke mid-sentence and asked.

"Operation Free The Frog," Dumby answered with a hint of pride in his eyes.

"Hmmm. That has a ring to it," Bilac said, and Dumby's chest became even more swollen. He couldn't help but keep on smiling.

"Who do we have with us? "

"As I said, Commander Lance Forsyth and his men. "Dumby continued, "The intelligence for the operation isn't the best. We could only do so much in such little time. "

"There are no excuses, Dumby, and you know that. "

Dumby closed his eyes, exasperated. He nodded but didn't address Bilac's reservation at once. Instead, he went on about the mission, 'Clean PJs,' and said, "The Delta planners have to rely on the reports of an Arab doctor who had been tending to Pierre Jean. From him, we learned where PJ was exactly located and the general layout of the Fleury-Mérogis Prison building, and also the surrounding town of Fleury-Mérogis, in the southern suburbs of Paris. "

"What's our informer's name? The asset on the ground at the Fleury-Mérogis?"

Dumby looked around and whispered to Bilac, "There are two of them, Beau Bastien Marat and Dr. Faiq Noah."

"What kind of a name is that?" Bilac frowned.

"He's a mix of two ethnicities, Belgian and Palestinian."

"All right. What about the Beau guy?"

"He's French, as French anyone can get, and both speak perfect English." He paused. "If you don't have someone in mind who will take over after PJ, we have two candidates ready."

"Oh, shut it, Dumby. Where'd you find these clowns?"

Dumby sustained, "Bilac, they're anything but clowns. The final plan is to land on the roof, breach the rooftop door, and descend two floors to reach PJ's cell. The assault force would then fly away on the Little Birds with their precious cargo."

"No, no, no, no."

"What's the matter? Delta Force's 2 Troop is given the task of rescuing PJ. Four MH-6 Little Bird helicopters from the 160th Special Operations Aviation Regiment, known as 'the Night Stalkers,' would land 23 Delta operators on the...."

"He's not supposed to be inside when the rescue team gets there," Bilac looked at Dumby, who shrugged. "We need him to be out in the courtyard, with minimal guards and a football game being broadcast on live television. We need as many distractions as we can come up with."

"Sure, okay, let me call Lance. Wait." Dumby picked up his phone from the table and dialed the colonel's number.

"Dumby, this guy of yours, the Special Forces guy...."

"Lance?"

"Yes, him. He knows that this is super confidential and must be hidden from both governments at all costs."

"I'm sure he does."

"What do you mean, you're sure he does?" Bilac was getting impatient. "Give me the damn phone."

"Wait, what do you want to tell him."

"Just gimme the phone, Dumby. Dial the colonel's number and give me your phone."

After twenty minutes or so, both Bilac and the colonel were

down to the actual modality of the rescue operation. "Delta Force's 2 Troop, A Squadron... Yeah"

"Four MH-6 Little Bird helicopters from the 160th Special Operations Aviation Regiment, known as the what?" he almost shouted into the mouthpiece.

"Oh, right, the 'Night Stalkers.'"

"They will land ten Delta operators on the prison's roof. Is that what you said, colonel?"

"I want them to land in the courtyard...."

"No, it doesn't matter. It's just French casualties. It doesn't matter. The collateral damage is meaningless in the face of our rescue operation, like always."

"All right, that 10.30 am sharp – right, okay, yes, I get you. Wait for me or Dumby to call you."

****

"I propose a shift in focus from the interior to the exterior spaces of the prison, specifically to prison surroundings." Dr. Faiq Noah kept speaking to himself as he wandered through the empty cell block A. "I aim to trace the role of prison surroundings by looking more closely at the prisoners' sensory perception of 'what goes on beyond 'its high walls' and how this affects their experience of imprisonment. Based on ethnographic data generated within the scope of a research project on indefinite confinement in Switzerland, providing insight into long-term prisoners' sensory perception of the outside world during two particular time-space constellations: while being locked up in the cell and during the daily one-hour walk in the courtyard.

"I argue that the sensory impressions of the outside world, which prisoners experience through the cell window or while being physically 'outside,' affect not only prisoners' understanding of 'the prison' but also their experience of time and their sense of self. A closer look at their diverse ways of managing these potential connections to the outside world reveals their approaches to the indefinite nature of their incarceration."

His words trailed off, falling silent as he came to an abrupt halt. His attention fixated on the procession of prisoners being guided by vigilant jail guards towards the distant courtyard, roughly fifty feet away. They were headed towards the South Wing of Cell Block A. A sense of anticipation filled the air, and with a whisper of resignation, he murmured, "Here we go."

****

Once both men were in the open field of the cemented-courtyard, both closed their eyes and took deep breaths. "Je regrette l'époque où j'habitais Paris et je pouvais rentrer dans les musées juste pour une heure, contempler une seule œuvre et repartir."[39]

"Vous n'avez pas à attendre longtemps,"[40] Beau Bastien Marat said to PJ, who looked at him puzzled.

---

[39] "I miss the days when I lived in Paris and could go into museums for just an hour, contemplate a single work and leave."
[40] "You don't have long to wait,"

"Comment ça, Marat?"[41] PJ asked him.

"J'entends presque le bruit des hélicos."[42]

"Hélicoptères? Je ne comprends pas."[43]

Both of them caught sight of a figure sprinting towards them from the entrance of Cell Block A, the very same door through which the prisoners had ventured into the courtyard for their allotted hour of respite. Dr. Faiq Noah, consumed by urgency, broke into a swift sprint, stealing occasional glances to his right. Above the towering walls of the penitentiary, his gaze seemed to be drawn to the expanse of the cloudless, cerulean sky. Closing the distance rapidly, he began speaking in rapid succession as soon as he reached the two men. Les Américains sont presque là!"

"Quoi, comment, qui?"[44] Pierre Jean asked him, frowning.

"Des Américains?"

"Pour quoi faire?"[45]

Beau Bastien Marat and Dr. Faiq Noah looked at each other, before the doctor spoke, "Ils t'emmènent loin d'ici."[46]

"Je m'envole? Où?"[47]

"Aux USA, ton frère te veut là-bas."[48]

---

[41] "What do you mean, Marat?"
[42] "I can almost hear the sound of helicopters."
[43] "Helicopters? I don't understand."
[44] "What, how, who?"
[45] "What's the point?"
[46] "They're taking you away from here."
[47] "I'm flying away? Where?"
[48] "To the States, your brother wants you there."

"Mon frère? What do you say and mean?"

"Do not play innocent you know the new American President is your brother?" Beau Bastien Marat said.

Pierre Jean did not respond. He kept looking at both their faces, shifting his glances from one to the other. "C'est tellement confus."[49]

With PJ's words lingering in the air, an undeniable sense of anticipation gripped the trio and those around them. Their gazes collectively ascended, their eyes fixated on the tranquil and balmy sky above. Suddenly, a metallic sound resonated from the very heart of the clouds, captivating their attention and punctuating the atmosphere with an otherworldly presence.

"C'est quoi ce bruit?"[50]

"That, my friend, is the sound of freedom."

"I do not understand," PJ was getting anxious. "What have you two planning?"

"We thought we'd get you a date for the prom, Peter," the doctor said.

Then it dawned on PJ, "Non, non, non, non!"

He started to walk towards the door that would lead him back inside the walls of the Fleury-Mérogis. Both men held him by the shoulder, and he almost lost footing but managed to balance at the last minute. The grinding sound became louder.

"Laissez-moi partir,"[51] PJ shouted to no avail. The men held

---

[49] "It's so confusing."
[50] "What's that noise?"
[51] "Let me go."

him in a tight hold.

"Désolé, mais c'est pour ton bien, PJ,"[52] the doctor said as a loud blade slap was heard directly above them.

The courtyard exploded into chaos as unmarked helicopters materialized into view. A swarm of small birds seemed to accompany them, filling the air with their flapping wings. Among the fleet, the Sikorsky HH-60 Pave Hawk—a combat and rescue aircraft—hovered menacingly over the jail's confines. Gradually, more of these formidable birds joined the airborne ensemble.

The deafening cacophony intensified as the thunderous roar of a GAU-18/A reverberated through the surroundings. Equipped with a 50-caliber machine gun, the weapon drowned out all other sounds, subduing everything within the vicinity of the three men. As dust billowed and swirled, miniature twisters formed in the courtyard, adding turmoil to the unfolding spectacle. Their garments danced wildly, especially the loose-fitting thoub worn by the doctor.

Amidst the pandemonium, the distinct clamor of 7.62mm NATO Miniguns being armed pierced through the chaos. In an instant, shots rang out, obliterating two watchtowers and the unfortunate guards stationed within them. The explosive impact further heightened the pandemonium, leaving an indelible mark on the scene unfolding before the astonished onlookers.

Inside one of the birds, a certain Captain Humbert Livingston spoke into his headpiece, "Come in, Hawker 1, come in. We are facing a free route environment. Please advise.

---

[52] "Sorry, but it's for your own good, PJ."

Breaker."

As he received directions from the US, he maneuvered the GAU-18/A and spoke again, "This is Operation Clean PJs. Deviation from procedures, provision detected outside the area of responsibility, skipping unnecessary coordination, breaker."

The bird made a turn as the French brought out their ground-to-air missile (GTAM) weapons and started to fire at the birds, which showed the intent of landing in the Fleury-Mérogis Prison courtyard.

A jolt of horror rippled through the onlookers as a French guard stationed at the GTAM, was struck directly in the face by a devastating projectile. The impact obliterated his visage, leaving nothing but a gruesome aftermath. Like a lifeless weight, the headless Frenchman plummeted to the ground.

"Putain! Il se passe quoi, bordel?"[53] PJ shouted. His voice could not be heard through the great commotion. Just then, the ground beside him was littered with 12 mm slugs. They made the dirt fly rise and settle. PJ and the other two jumped.

"What is wrong with those Yankees? Why are they shooting at us?" Beau Bastien Marat shouted.

"What the fuck is wrong with you, Staff Sergeant Jonah?" Captain Humbert Livingston asked the gunner as he saw what the idiot had just done, "You almost tore the asset into a million pieces, boy."

Jonah did not reply.

With the chopper finally touching down, the fellow inmates rallied together, swiftly springing into action to assist in the

---

[53] "Fuck! What the fuck is going on?"

evacuation. They carefully guided and placed PJ Labaguette into one of the awaiting aircraft, amidst the tumultuous backdrop of the transformed jail courtyard. What was once a confined space had now become a fierce battleground, as a relentless exchange of fire ensued between the jail guards and the descending choppers. In their resolute pursuit, the choppers systematically dismantled the French jail security, amplifying the chaos that engulfed the scene.

"Je ne veux pas y aller."[54]

"Too late for that, PJ, have a great trip, and say hi to Angelina Jolie from me," Dr. Faiq Noah said, smiling.

Marat bade him farewell as the French authorities opened fire on the chopper and the three men. Marat was hit in the back and fell to the ground. He coughed blood. And felt on the ground. The doctor, PJ, and the pilot saw this, and Captain Livingston pulled on the cyclic stick, making the chopper ascend steeply. PJ was half inside with the men inside the chopper trying to pull him on board, and the doctor tried to push his legs when a French bullet hit him.

One of the crew members handed him a helmet and a headset, "Put those on, now."

PJ did just that, as the noise disappeared, and after a little while, it returned but only as a weak hum. "Will the man be okay?"

"Oh, he'll be fine as a fiddle," the crew smiled, knowing well that the doc was probably dead by now. After all, they had blown his lower half to smithereens, and this idiot had the nerve

---

[54] "I don't want to go."

to ask if he was okay. What a turd!

****

Several miles and hours later, Pierre Jean was in the south of France. Captain Humbert Livingston, Commander Lance Forsyth, and Staff Sergeant Jonah had landed the Bell H-13 Sioux (M*A*S*H television series was a Bell H-13 Sioux, the U.S. Army equivalent of the Bell 47D-1), with the 'package' at the Paris Charles de Gaulle

The captain landed his 'small bird' at a secret helipad, which was at the east wing of the Aéroports de Paris (Group ADP) and out of sight of the general public and even most people from the government and the army or the French Air Force, this was the place where the birds landed after every clandestine operation, they moved PJ to a commercial chopper

****

The helicopter took them to a in a few miles in land from Nice a niche and an exclusive area. Because of complete privacy,

The villa was built away from the crowd, at a location that was hard to reach, and it also exuded a sense of luxury. The villa had eight rooms with attached bathrooms and comfortable and spacious living space. In the front was a huge compound where many flowers were planted. The looming structure was made of wood, tiles, and marble. The floor was completely made of jade marble. Each of the bedrooms was large, airy, and well-lit.

The toilets were big, with all modern fixtures installed,

including the rain shower, a giant bathtub, a jacuzzi, and what have you. The dining hall was beautifully decorated with a chandelier that hung from the high ceiling, mahogany furniture, and exclusive, vintage China in expensive wooden cabinets with non-reflective glass. The kitchen looked upon a small forest, and the scenery was breathtaking, with rabbits frequenting the place.

This included courts for lawn sports, jogging paths, manicured parks, an outdoor Jacuzzi adjacent to the pool.

With its own 24/7 monitoring services. The property was safe and fully protected by private guards.

After spending an entire day in the room, Pierre Jean became restless. He started calling repeatedly, asking to be let out, when he found out that his door was locked from the outside. "Let me get out of here."

"I'm afraid I cannot do that, sir." That was the response he was getting true the door.

"What can you do?" PJ asked, fuming at the ears.

"Well, Mr. Vincent Cassel, can I put you on hold, sir?"

"No, I'm in a holding cell in France, then I'm in a holding cell in whomever this place is my name is not Cassel."

The villa staff was not authorized to engage PJ in any conversation except for ordering food and fresh laundry. They were strictly told that they would be committing a criminal offense if they let the occupant of the master bedroom know where he was or anything other detail of his stay.

"You're in a safe place, Mr. Cassel." The guy on the phone paused, then resumed, "soon, you will have some company.

Please let them in. One of those is a staff who will help you with the use of the jacuzzi.

"I don't want a f.... jacuzzi!" PJ shouted into the phone. "I want to see my children."

"Yes, but of course, Mr. Cassel." The room service hung up.

After a while, PJ was in the Jacuzzi, buzzing with the effect of the drug and alcohol he had been served just after he arrived.

After the passage of thirty minutes, a few men and women gathered around the pool.

"Yes, who are those?" PJ stuck his head out of the water. He saw the group of people and did not recognize anyone.

As soon as he lifted his head, he was surprised to see two women who looked as if they had walked out of the pages of the Playboy magazine. Well, not just pages but the centerfold. Both looked like porn stars. A tall, muscular man in sunglasses accompanied them.

"Hi, I'm Sandra," one of the ladies said. She looked like a Latino and had an accent.

PJ only nodded as he ogled her huge breasts.

"Hey, handsome, they call me Ophelia," the other woman said. Later PJ found out that the tall, dark young, and extremely beautiful lady was from Africa, and Sandra was from Colombia.

"Can we go there with you?" Sandra asked, pointing at the jacuzzi.

PJ nodded again. He absolutely did not know that the women had been sent by the same people who were behind his escape/kidnapping. That they had been 'planted' there with a single purpose, not only to stroke and swallow and take PJ's carnality inside but a purpose more sinister. Yes, more sinister than fornication. Their main purpose was to seduce and have the President's brother's situation compromised.

"Did anyone tell you that you look exactly like the President of the United States!" Ophelia said as PJ let the women in.

Unbeknownst to PJ and the women, a photographer and videographer were taking pictures and making a Piere Labaguette sex tape. The women and PJ did not notice a drone hovering in the park, where the jacuzzi was, PJ was too excited to make anything of it. The women were taking everything in a stride. They had been paid well to keep their mouths shut and open.

"Yesterday I was in hell with ugly inmates trying to make me their girlfriend, and now I am in heaven with two angels," PJ took a deep breath and, smiled, and rested his back against the side of the jacuzzi. "God is with me. My brother is the most powerful man in this world."

He looked at Sandra. "I love him," He turned to Ophelia and looked at both the girls. "And I love you too."

He raised his glass of champagne towards the bodyguards, acting cool and distant, "And to you too, whoever you are, I love you too."

The guards looked at him and resumed looking elsewhere.

Sandra whispered to the other girl, "He is so sweet," she reached under the water "It sure looks like he hasn't had sex for months," they both snickered.

"W... What?" PJ asked, half smiling.

"Nothing, babe," Sandra dismissed his question and came closer.

The drone was taking pictures right before the trio, a mesh of sweat and flesh slithered in the bubbling jacuzzi. Everything was being seen by the Republicans who hatched the plan from the Republican Headquarters in Buffalo.

12

Identity Crisis

"No one knows better than a mom and dad how to take care of their kids."

— Former New Jersey Gov. Chris Christie

Sylvie stormed into Jean Pierre's office, disregarding the security guard's presence. She appeared disheveled, with no makeup and unruly hair. Wearing a nightgown and slippers, she seemed to be in disarray.

"Jean Pierre, Jean Pierre, my love, I need to speak to you

alone, please."

The president ordered everybody out and muted the cameras.

"What is wrong, my love? You ate some bad food?"

"No," she whispered. "It is Patrick," she cried louder and collapsed in the presidential chair.

"Call a doctor. We have a medical staff in the white house," he said as he ran to his cell phone.

"No love, he is not sick, or shall I say he may be sick, but a different sickness or I do not know, maybe it is normal."

"Explain me. I am confused," The President said as he took her hands and kissed her palms.

"He wants to become a girl ..."

"Patrick, our soccer player, our karate champion, wants to become a girl." He took his head in his hand and glanced through the window, repeating, "Patrick wants to be a girl. My son wants to be a girl. My little macho wants to change sex."

JP served himself a drink and offered one to his wife.

She refused, "I cannot eat. I cannot drink. I am devastated and puzzled."

"Me too."

She breathed heavily as she heaved, "He wants to be called Patsy."

"My God. I am elected. I do not need the votes of LBGTABCDE, etc..."

"Let us keep it in the family. I will talk to him."

"Her," replied Sylvie

"Her. You are right. Patsy, at least it is not too far from Patrick."

"He chooses it."

"Yes, she did."

She squeezed him and whispered, "And there is more."

"She wants to be pregnant?" he whispered back.

"No, this is about Jacqueline"

"I knew she would not accept it; girls are very jealous of each other and compete for dresses and bags." "We can deal with that. We will take them shopping in Paris."

"No, my love, this is not that."

"She is upset. I am upset. We can explain to her that it will take time, but we will all adapt." He took another drink and handed one to Sylvie. Please drink. Let us toast the rainbow house."

She sipped as she whispered, "Jean Pierre, Jacqueline wants to be a boy."

Jean Pierre turned white and collapsed on the floor.

"My daughter, my princess, my queen, my little Kardashian wants to be a boy! Jacqueline wants to be called Jack.

He went to vomit in the bathroom, and his gargles echoed. Sylvie winced. She rushed to the washroom, wiped his face, and knelt.

"OK, OK, nobody will see anything. We will still have a boy and a girl; nobody will see the difference as they are twins. "I just need to negotiate with them their name change."

"Just hope they do not want to change color!"

"Does Patrick want to become whiter and Jacqueline more black?" he asked with fear in his voice.

"No, my love, and maybe we should not give the idea! Just the name changes, and we are OK."

A wide smile appeared on Sylvie's face.

"My love, Mr. President, you are such a smart politician. I admire you. You find solutions for America and your family. I adore you. I will always be on your side." She finished his drink, kissed him with a smile, and left the room.

She glided past the vigilant guards with an air of serene confidence, her every step a testament to her unwavering devotion. "Our President is not just a leader," she declared, her voice carrying the weight of absolute conviction. "He's a visionary genius, and my beloved husband whom I adore with all my heart." With a tender smile, she embraced each guard, leaving a trail of warmth, sophistication and French perfume in her wake. "He tackles crises with the finesse of a master chef flipping crepes," she added, her words painting a vivid picture of his unparalleled skill and resolve. And with that, she moved forward, leaving behind a lingering aura of loyalty, admiration, and unwavering support.

13

The Scandal

"Any man worth his salt will stick up for what he believes right, but it takes a slightly better man to acknowledge instantly and without reservation that he is in error."

— Andrew Jackson

Sylvie Labaguette, growing increasingly confident and self-assured, took it upon herself to rename the Oval Office as the 'Croissant Office,' inspired by the changes in its shape and layout.

As twilight settled, JP and Sylvie shared a meal and ordinary chatter. Yet, as the night deepened, their conversation took a profound turn, delving into philosophy and existential wonder realms. What started as routine transformed into a captivating exchange of thoughts and ideas, enriching their evening with unexpected depth and insight.

The new White House chef, Fête Nationale, stood next to Sylvie. The First Lady had initially encountered the Haitian Chef on Instagram. They had begun corresponding once Sylvie decided to try his line of Haitian condiments. Sylvie was glad she did because he was a gem, and his food was delicious. Fête Nationale was happy to speak with Sylvie about his desire to highlight Haitian cuisine in the United States.

The cook brought a plate on the table

"What is it asked the president?"

"Chicken voodoo one of my compositions very aphrodisiac" replied the Fête Nationale

"Delicious" replied JP "let me indulge in another serving."

Sylvie stormed into the Croissant Office. Amidst her overwhelming emotions, she cried out loudly, showing immense distress. She turned on the television, only to find that most American news channels were airing a sex tape, preceded by a statutory warning about its explicit nature. The content displayed a graphic ménage à trois involving Peter Jean and two stunning, 'barely legal' girls named Sandra, the Colombian beauty, and Ophelia, the African goddess... The broadcast captivated viewers across the US, and its reach extended to half the world."

"Comment as-tu pu nous faire ça, on avait tout pour être

heureux?"[55]

Sylvie picked a dinner plate and flung it at JP, who ducked just in time. The plate crashed against the brick wall behind him.

"Tu m'as humilié moi et ma famille"[56]

JP watched the news first with eyes that were fully open and wide awake. His jaw almost touched the dinner table. "What the hell is going on here? There? Qu'est-ce que c'est?[57]"

His team, all of the king's men, had their eyes glued to the television. They all watched the different channels that played the steamy footage of PJ with the bimbos.

Jacob Hardy, one of the President's security advisors, said, "Look, Mr. President, they have footage of you in the company of who.... post, er, gir... er, women." The gentleman with dark hair perspired profusely, with beads of sweat trickling down his forehead. Despite the central air conditioning and cold, provided by floor-standing air conditioners throughout the place, he had formed dark circles of sweat under his armpits on his shirt.

The thermostat had to be adjusted, but not right away. Right now, the cold was necessary as tempers flared, and the climate at the Croissant House became hot as hell.

Jean Pierre couldn't believe what he was seeing and felt a surge of rage. "My clown of a brother, Peter..." He paused, wiping his brow, then glanced at Sylvie, half-expecting her to hurl something else at him—perhaps the fridge or the Ruud Central tower AC. "Qu'est-ce qu'il veut, un poste

---

[55] "How could you do that to us? We had everything to be happy?"
[56] "You humiliated me and my family."
[57] "What rubbish is this?"

d'ambassadeur? Me faire chanter pour de l'argent?"[58]

Jean Pierre suddenly jumped on the table with force and screamed as the table creaked under him. "This is not me," He shouted. "This is my idiot twin brother!" After which, Jean Pierre called his head of staff, General Michael D. Rooney, "Rooney."

"Yes, Mr. President?"

"Bring the Secret Service, and we must my brother and bring him to the US justice."

"Let me prepare a press release and arrange a press conference," Rooney said in a sullen voice.

The following day the press release was chartered in the Croissant Office. JPB declared to everyone in attendance, "I did not sleep with these women!" He looked at the fully packed room, "I will proof mine; what you call?"

"Innocence," Dumby assisted.

"Yes, I will proofread my innocence. What?" He looked at Bilac standing to his right and said something.

"Not proofread, prove, it's 'prove,' JP!"

"Qui ça intéresse que tu baises?"[59]

"What?"

"Enough! Shut it down!" JP retorted as he turned to face the individuals from the press who held the power to shape the minds of the American people and the world. Their decisions and influence would determine JP's fate, and he knew his future

---

[58] "What does he want an ambassador post, extort my money?"
[59] "Who cares, you fuck?"

lay in the hands of this audience."

"Your president is addicted to good food and his beautiful wife," JP said as he took Sylvie's hand. "Not porn stars and drugs."

"This man is not me this is my twin brother"

He pulled his pants down and showing his brother anatomy on the TV screen he shouted

"Look at the difference"

The audience members started to talk among themselves. Some raised their hands to ask questions, but JP waved them off, "No interrogation; I'm your bloody president; I'm not crook."

"Like Nixon?" A lady from CNN said.

"What are you talking about? I said no investigations."

"Nothing, nothing, pardon me, sir," she said, exchanging a look with her colleagues, reporters, and journalists. They were all smiling, yet some were frowning and upset at seeing a true laughingstock as their President.

Sylvie left in tears and walked toward the pool she met the pool boy watching the news.

In the pool room, Sylvie jumped on him started to have sex while the TV was on a little far from the pool area. Sylvie was moaning and cuddling the pool boy. Sergio the pool boy looked at the TV and lost his concentration, upon which the first lady said, "What is happening? You are now a soft baby snake, she smiled.

The pool boy looked at his penis and the screen, "I am so sorry."

Sylvie fed oysters to the pool boy, who spat it out. "Oysters, why oysters?"

"It will make you strong, my boy."

"You told me you are now a vegetarian?"

"Yes, but you must not be; you must be a strong Latin lover – Mon amour fait moi l'Amour"[60]

"I need strong Latin music. I cannot have sex without music."

"No, my love. We need to be discreet." Sylvie inserted air pods in his ears and went down on him. He smiled, "I love oysters."

****

The president had left the conference room and met with Fête Nationale.

"Where is my wife?"

"I do not know Mr. President"

"That tape of my brother made me so stormy and you chicken voodoo is acting on me."

"I need sex"

"But Sir"

"Now! I am the president"

"I know a place we can go," Fête said.

"My favorite swinger club is close by, and you will not be

---

[60] "My love makes me Love."

recognized."

"Why?"

"We all wear masks. The girls are beautiful and willing," he licked his lips.

"My god, that powerful stuff you put in the chicken! I'm painting the downside. How do we get there, pretending to be somebody else?"

"I have a scooter. Let's go. Our girls will wait at the swingers' club door."

They escaped on a scooter. The Secret Service tried to catch them without success.

Once they reached the 'Better than your Wife cheaper than a Divorce Club,' Fête took JP to a VIP room and gave him a gown and a Clinton mask. Fête wore a mask of Trump.

They walked through the club, where people engaged in depraved sexual acts. Two beautiful girls walked toward them. The "hostesses" went down on their knees and performed fellatio on them both.

"Thank you, Mr. President," One of the girls said, wiping the cum off her eyes and mouth.

"Mr. President, what do you mean? who told you? Please keep quiet; my lawyer will contact you, and we will sign a confidentiality agreement."

"Mr. President, we recognized you from the press conference footage about the sex tape ".

They giggled. Fête Nationale intervened, "Everything is okay?"

"The girls recognized me," JP sounded alarmed.

"No problem, let me talk to them."

Fête went to talk to them and returned after a while.

Immediately, JP asked him, "Did you work a deal?"

"Yes, we can use some hush money you owe me one more time," he proclaimed, laughing under his Trump mask.

"What do you want, my greedy friend?"

"Haiti."

"Let us open some chicken voodoo restaurants in the meantime it's less complicated."

"I want to become the President of Haiti" he begged.

"Easy, let's do it" smiled JP.

The following day he called his generals.

"We are gone invade Haiti and my friend here will be elected" he winked.

"Yes, Mr. President, will start the process immediately, what is the new president of Haiti name?"

JP turned toward Fête Nationale

"Fête Nationale?"

"No Uncle Doc, will be my name."

"And Mr. President can I get another favor?"

"What is it my friend?"

"Can I get Saint Barth as well?" whispered the soon to be elected Haitian president.

"No impossible this is already a Russian Colony."

"Let us go. I have a lot of work to do, and thanks to your stormy friends, I feel terrific."

****

They returned to the Blue, White, and Red House and were stopped at the entrance. The President lifted his helmet, and they were allowed inside.

13

Haiti

"The chief of the tribe is supposed to be the father of all people of the tribe. That is the Haitian way."

— Francois Duvalier

Shouting at his generals, JP yelled, "Get ready, and we are going invade Haiti." Fête Nationale was on the podium holding hands with the President.

Republicans said, "Now what? Look at the pool. All the Haitians are going to support them."

JP announced, "And I introduce the new President of Haiti, 'Uncle Doc.'

****

In a secluded place in Haiti, some thugs with hostages were watching the television.

"Liberate the hostages. We are fucked. They are gone bring back the Tonton Macoutes and the US Army."

The gangsters liberated the hostages and gave them money. "Sorry, we made a mistake. We apologize"

The hostage said, "Thanks, but this is gourdes. Don't you have dollars?" The thugs look at each other

"You will not talk, "you swear. Okay?" The chief of the criminals named Barbecue gave his Rolex and gold chain.

In Haiti, people were cheering in the streets. Uncle Doc was on the Haitian National TV.

"I will vindicate the principles of peace and justice in the life of Haiti."

Uncle Doc went to JP's office after the press conference. "Thank you, Mr. President."

****

14

Assassination

It is hard to fail, but it is worse never to have tried to succeed. In this life, we get nothing save by effort.

— Theodore Roosevelt

The Republicans were discussing how to get rid of Jean Pierre as the sex scandal did not succeed. One of the Republicans said, "We need to poison his food, we need to assassinate him. We need to do something, goddammit."

"Havana Syndrome," one of the Hawks said.

"We have a Cuban prisoner, Jose. He is a specialist in microwave technology. He worked on the Havana syndrome."

"Jean Pierre will experience dizziness, loss of balance, hearing loss, anxiety, and something similar to a 'cognitive fog'."

"You mean like Biden Bilac said sarcastically."

"Yes, exactly."

"How do we do that?"

"We hire Jose as a cleaner. We put him in a janitor's room next to the President's office and provided the material. Risky, but possible we can get him clearance papers and promise him a reduction of jail time or send him back to Cuba."

"Is that dangerous for the rest of the staff? The Secret Service may be affected," Dumby looked concerned.

"Jose tells us he can focus the radiation on a limited, pre-calculated area."

"Let's give it a shot," GW said, got up, and left the room.

After a few weeks, Jose had his clearance and access to his private janitorial room. He smuggled small electronic parts and started to build his Havana Syndrome apparatus.

In the following weeks, Jean Pierre appeared happier and more energetic, as he told his staff, "There is such good energy in the Blue-White and Red House.

In a secret meeting in the safe house, the furious Republicans interviewed Jose.

"What are you doing? Jean Pierre was supposed to have symptoms."

Jose said, "Quien es Jean Pierre?"

"What the fuck, our president, the one you were hired to terminate."

Jose held his head in his hands, "Disculpe tengo dolor de la cabeza muy fuerte."[61]

He stood up and dropped like a fly.

The Republicans were furious. "This moron eradicated himself!"

"Yo Jose, get the fuck up. Hey, Jose," Bilac snapped his fingers. Dumby splashed water on his face from a bottle of Evian. "We are sending you to Cuba."

"Usted es de viaje a Guantanamo

"You are traveling to Guantanamo Cuba. "

Jose seemed to be having a brain fog. "Cuba¿ Donde es Cuba."

"Cuba Where is Cuba."

"I cannot see this jerk."

****

Poisoning

In a dark office under heavy security, a gentleman came into the Republican Headquarters. Jerry and Ted started interviewing him.

"Hello, how are you?"

"I'm well," answered the gentleman with a Russian accent.

---

[61] "Excuse me, I have a terrible headache."

"Your name is Igor?"

"I know."

"I'm asking you; you fool."

"Как ты смеешь называть меня дураком

"How dare you call me a fool?"

"You were in London on the sixteenth of October, 2006?"

"Maybe"

Jerry placed a suitcase full of money on the table. "This is to jog your memory, Igor."

"Yes, I was."

"Were you in London on the twenty-fifth of October?"

"Maybe?" Igor did not make eye contact; instead, he looked out the single window in the office.

They put another suitcase full of money on the table.

"я вспомнила... I mean, I remember."

"Were you in the Millennium Hotel in Grosvenor Square on the first of November?"

Igor was stuck on repeat unless a suitcase was placed on the table: "Maybe."

They put another suitcase on the table and slammed it down. Igor was startled, but he finally made eye contact.

"Yes, nice hotel, I remember now," Igor answered.

"Can you help us to eliminate somebody without messing up the environment?" Bilac asked Igor.

"Do you have polonium available?" Dumby added.

Igor repeated what he's been repeating since grade two, "Maybe."

This time, there was no suitcase; instead, Jerry slammed a loaded Glock onto the table, "Does this refresh your memory?"

"I... I remember," said Igor. "We have more experience, and we will use a smaller dose in a drink, maybe tea. It will work."

"How are we going to have JP drink that tea?'

"Dr. Gueleman hates JP," Igor continued, "JP never takes his medications. JP wants only natural medications."

"Dr. Gueleman is a strong Republican and will help us."

They all shook hands and toasted with Grey Goose Vodka.

"Here's to fascism!"

"да здравствует фашизм

"Long live fascism."

They called Doctor Gueleman, and they had tea boxes prepared within a week. They asked the good doctor if he could help the Hawks make JP consume some of that tea daily.

"He never does what I tell him, but I will try," said Dr. Gueleman.

Bialac was getting impatient, "How do we know it will work?"

"Vomiting, diarrhea, then he will lose his hair."

"We had similar promises from our Cuban expert."

****

175

After a few weeks, JP had a haircut. The hairdresser told him, "Mr. President, how your hair is growing is incredible."

His manicurist agreed, "Mr. President, your nails are so strong and growing every week!"

JP was in fantastic shape. He told his team that he felt outstanding.

"I think it is thanks to this tea," he said as he showed the Russian-made tea to them.

"Excellent," JP said and offered some to Bilac. "I endorse it." Can a President endorse products?"

"The Royal family of England can, we cannot," he added.

A Few Days Later...

"Jerry, find me, Igor. That guy is a Russian spy. They are not conscientious," Bilac said impatiently.

"Oh, you mean the French and the Americans are?" Dumby snickered.

"Cut the crap and get me that Russian expert now."

For several days, they could not locate Igor. Finally, they found him, somehow. He was in the Mercy Hospital of Buffalo. He had no more hair. It was as if he had become skinny overnight.

"Igor, what did you do? JP is getting better. And look at you. What did you do? How much polonium did you put in his tea?"

Igor managed to utter, "I used homoeopathic doses."

****

Back at the Republican party, Bilac told his cohorts that Igor fucked up, "We need to get rid of him."

"The hospital called me, and he is dead," Dumby said as he rubbed his chin.

Jerry said, "We need a pansy. An Oswald?"

"Lee Harvey Oswald?"

"No, Oswald Cobblepot, you dimwit."

****

The Sicarios

"Let's get some Colombian hitmen. They are the best. Find them some motorbikes without plates," Bilac ordered his men.

In an obscure office, Pablo and Henrique, with biker helmets on their heads, negotiated with the Hawks. They had a strong Medellin accent. "You think you can do it?" Jerry asked.

"Puess Claro que sí, Señor, nosotros somos los mejores sicarios aquí. Esta es mi hoja de vida,"[62] Pablo responded with assertiveness...

Jerry looked at the list. "Impressive, and you were never indicted?" he inquired.

They both laughed, "By whom? Judges do not want to die!" Henrique remarked.

---

[62] "Well of course we are, sir, we are the best hit men here. This is my resume."

Jerry decided to step out of the situation, "I cannot deal with these guys anymore; make a deal with them, Ted."

****

The following week, JP was riding his Peugeot e-Ludix electric scooter with a security phalanx on both sides, and personnel were riding a 2016 Harley Davidson Road King and 2015 Street Glide with Visor. Suddenly, two BMW R1200 RT-P police motorcycles appeared and drove toward JP.

All security guards began to prepare themselves to shoot, but the sicarios were fast. They closed in from the left and right sides. They had JP in their crosshairs and started shooting. JP deliberately slid off his scooter as it skidded across the asphalt, and both sicarios hit each other in the face and died in the crossfire.

JP walked back to his scooter, picked it up, got on it, and continued to ride. He called one of his men, "Remind me to change the gun laws when I have some time."

****

15

Indictment or Impeachment

*We could very well have a sitting president under felony
indictment and ultimately a criminal trial."*

— Donald Trump

****

"Current procedures have raised the question of whether a
president can be indicted while in office or is immune from
criminal prosecution."

"It has never happened before," Jasper Courtney, the special aide to Senator Ted Dumby, said. "The text of the Constitution is unclear, and there are respectable opinions on both sides where we try to deal with the situation at hand."

Gloria Winston, the president's speechwriter, said, "Today, we are talking about whether a sitting president can be criminally indicted."

"This permissible notion becomes germane every twenty years, starting with President Nixon, moving on to President Clinton, and now potentially Jean Pierre Labaguette." Dumby added, "But first, there's the difference between indictment and impeachment."

"Enlighten us, Dumby," Bilac said sarcastically, and his mouth broke into a half-smile.

"An indictment is a criminal charge against an individual." Dumby paused, looked around, and found James Bullard, president and CEO of the Federal Reserve Bank of St. Louis, eyeing him. Dumby became a little nervous. He continued, "It is essentially how you initiate criminal prosecuting. So, for example, if someone murdered another person, the state would prosecute that individual for manslaughter."

"On the other hand, impeachment is a purely political instrument to remove an official from the federal government. Right?" Democrat Richard Bordeaux interrupted Dumby.

"It is a formal charge of wrongdoing and potentially removing them from office," Bordeaux finished and looked at Dumby.

"But unlike an indictment, it does not necessarily result in jail time," Gloria Winston added.

"In popular parlance, impeachment generally refers to the

president, but it can refer to a wide variety of federal government employees," Clara Mayfield, the Congresswoman from Milwaukee, said. "Most of the impeachments involve Supreme Court justices, not just the President of the United States."

Bilac jumped in, "So you might ask, why would anyone think the president is immune from prosecution?"

"First, let's recognize that most government officials are immune from suits to allow them to focus on their jobs as elected officials." Attorney General Samuel Peterson was also among the plotters. The mantra was a 'friend to Jean Pierre's enemy is a foe to the US.' The Hawks and the Doves sat together at the GOP headquarters in Buffalo after VP Bilac called for this secret meeting.

The Attorney general continued, "For example, the doctrine of qualified immunity protects officials from facing criminal charges or lawsuits for their actions as long as they are within the course and scope of their jobs. Qualified immunity is often a defense raised in suits against police officers or police departments. Additionally, looking at the text of the Constitution, you'll notice that it does mention impeachment of the president, but it does not mention indictment."

James Bullard, president and CEO of the Federal Reserve Bank of St. Louis, was also present in the same room where the presidential campaigning for JP began, "An absence of that statement does not necessarily mean that it's not available." He removed his glasses and wiped them with a handkerchief he carried, something like a pocket square, but Bullard had removed his suit jacket and pulled out the pochette from one of the pockets in the trousers. He continued, "There's ambiguity in the Constitution."

"This is why the Office of Legal Counsel has dealt with this topic several times!" Samuel Peterson exclaimed.

"Hate to say this, Honorable Attorney General...." Dumby said.

"Please call me Peterson."

"Mr. Peterson, generally, it's seen as a non-partisan office. When the president has a question of law, they turn to the OLC to give an objective opinion." Dumby looked toward Bilac, who was intensely looking at Richard Bordeaux, another congressman from the Democrat's side.

"Relevant here, the OLC has written three memos on whether the president can be criminally indicted," Bordeaux put a pencil back into his mouth as he finished talking.

"If I'm not wrong, the first OLC memo was issued in 1973, shortly before the Saturday Night Massacre in which Nixon fired Watergate Special Prosecutor Archibald Cox, and the top two Justice officials resigned in protest."

Bordeaux took the pencil from his mouth, "That memo considers the Constitution's text and finds no answer. It finds that the Constitution provides very limited immunities for members of Congress and none for the president."

"Isn't that good?" Gloria Winston said, "I shouldn't care, but here I am, officially sacked by the man himself."

"That can be challenged," Bilac said confidently.

Gloria looked at Bilac, and he winked at her. She looked away.

"With no clear constitutional answer, the OLC lawyers asked what answer would best serve the nation?" Bordeaux said. "They found that an indictment in office would besmirch the 'symbolic head of the nation,' and given that impeachment is the only tool mentioned in the Constitution, the memo finds that this would suggest strongly that criminal proceedings against a president in office should not go beyond the point that would effectively remove the president and thus become a shortcut to impeachment."

"That's Catch-22," Dumby muttered.

"Your asshole plan was the motherlode of all Catch-22s. What are you talking about, Congressman Dumby?" Bullard scoffed at Ted.

"A second memo was written just a few days later by Robert Bork argues that the same points apply to the vice president as well."

"Who? What? Me?" Bilac almost jumped from his chair.

"You should know better, Mr. Vice President."

"No more, I quit."

"This isn't exactly a good time," Clara Mayfield said.

"But guys, those memos were never tested," Gloria raised her hands to fix her ponytail. "President Nixon resigned before either impeachment or indictment and was pardoned by President Ford."

"Twenty-seven years later, in 2000, the OLC reexamined the question." Clara Mayfield added, "By this time, there had been major Supreme Court decisions, all indicating that the president was, in fact, not immune to the justice system's reach." She took a deep breath, poured herself some water from the Evian bottle, and continued. "But the OLC found that despite case law, the president was still immune from criminal prosecution."

Bullard poignantly brought an essential point to everyone's consideration, "The OLC memo from the year 2000 states that the framers considered who should possess the extraordinary power of deciding whether to initiate a proceeding that could remove the president and placed that responsibility in the elected officials of Congress."

He went on to describe the status quo. "It would be inconsistent with that carefully considered judgment to permit an unelected grand jury and prosecutor to effectively remove a president by bringing criminal charges against him while he remains in office."

"That means, once again, that a sitting president could not be criminally indicted," Bilac sounded forlorn.

"At least not while in office," Dumby tried to console him.

"But you should probably consider the bias of these particular sources," Congresswoman Clara Mayfield said. "The three no-indictment opinions were issued by executive branch lawyers who work for the president."

"Of course, it has been noted that the Department of Justice has an active policy of not indicting a sitting president." Samuel Peterson stated, "However, this is a policy preference of the Department of Justice, and no one argues that the Constitution or statute mandates it."

"It may or may not be a good idea, but there is no law that requires this particular DOJ policy," Courtney said, and Bullard looked at her, impressed.

"She's right." Bullard said, "This DOJ policy and those memos from the Office of Legal Counsel may be well-reasoned, but none are binding. The final answer may come to us specifically from the United States Supreme Court."

"And if we're talking about the Supreme Court...." Bilac started.

"We should look at past Supreme Court precedent," The Congresswoman from Milwaukee said.

****

16

JPL Tried to Save His Presidency

"The only thing we have to fear is fear itself."

— **Franklin D. Roosevelt**

Jean Pierre Labaguette found himself sitting alone in one of the 132 rooms of the Georgian mansion, still clad in his jammies. The elegant architecture of the mansion followed the Palladian style, exuding an air of grandeur. Lost in contemplation, he perched on his bed, immersed in profound thoughts. The five o'clock shadow had now evolved into a day-old growth, the evidence of stubble forming a nascent beard.

For days, Jean-Paul had neglected the most straightforward personal care routines - no showering or shaving. He had become privy to the clandestine plans and schemes hatched by those who had once brought him into power. The same people who had seemingly relished dining at his renowned restaurants now revealed their true intentions, plotting behind his back. The betrayal left him disillusioned, questioning the authenticity of their past camaraderie.

He felt betrayed and sad. He muttered something to himself, "C'étaient les mêmes personnes en qui j'avais confiance." [63]

"With a heavy heart, Jean Pierre lowered his head, letting it hang low, almost touching the upper part of his chest. His arms found solace on the queen-sized bed, and he absentmindedly wiggled his toes, alternating between them, one foot on top of the other. A profound sense of distress and unease weighed heavily on him, leaving him feeling distraught and on edge.

JP looked up and gazed out of one of the windows directly onto the south of the house, bordered on the east by the East Executive Drive and the Treasury.

"Comment peuvent-ils faire ça?" [64] He looked at the vast landscape almost entirely of grass, or so it seemed from JP's vantage point, from where it was all uphill.

Jean Pierre's hand clenched into a tight fist, opening momentarily before regaining its grip. His thoughts were consumed by gloom and doom, channeling his dejection into vengeful fantasies of retribution against those who plotted

---

[63] "These were the same people I trusted with my life."
[64] "How can they do this?"

against him. He envisioned chopping the heads of all the men and women involved in the conspiracy. Though he knew only Bilac and Dumby's names for sure, he assumed more people were aiding the two Republicans in their machinations. The scale of the task ahead seemed daunting, requiring many co-conspirators to pull off such a scheme.

As these thoughts raced through his mind, Jean Pierre's hand tightly gripped the bedsheet, crumpling the fabric.

The atmosphere across America was filled with an outcry and backlash against Jean Pierre Labaguette, with countless people holding banners and placards expressing their grievances. Phrases like 'Remove the Clown,' 'Better dead than Fed,' and 'Let the French handle JPL!' echoed throughout the nation, lamenting him as their President.

Overwhelmed with emotions, Jean Pierre felt tears welling up. His thoughts drifted to Sylvie and her affair with the pool boy.

The TV had been running on mute all this time. JP reached for the remote control and hit the volume button. A man in his early fifties, wearing a dapper suit with salt and pepper hair, could be seen on screen. He had a stern expression as he said, "There are at least as many ways to abuse power as the powers vested in the President. It would thus be an exercise in futility to attempt a list of every abuse of power constituting 'high Crimes and Misdemeanors.'

"That said, impeachable abuse of power can be engaging in official acts forbidden by law and engaging in official action with motives prohibited by law.

The handsome newscaster continued, "This warning

echoed Edmund Randolph's teaching that impeachment must be allowed because 'the Executive will have great opportunities of abusing his power.'

President Richard Nixon's conduct has come to exemplify impeachable abuse of power: he acted with corrupt motives in obstructing justice and using official power to target his political opponents, and his decision to unlawfully defy subpoenas issued by the House impeachment inquiry was unconstitutional on its face."

Jean Pierre shut the television and hurled the remote in the air as he let out a primal grunt. The remote flew toward a table lamp and knocked it down. "What the hell is going around?" Jean Pierre screamed into the empty room.

Just then, there was a knock at the door. It startled Jean Pierre and made him jump, "Who is there? What do you want?"

"Open the door, Mr. Labaguette. This is the FBI," a voice spoke.

"Mr. Labaguette? Nobody is calling me that. It is Mr. President, OK?" JP shouted back.

"Open the door now, or we will have to break it open," The same voice resumed, barking orders to the President or ex-president. The voice on the other side of the door was instinctual and natural but highly severe and professional.

"All right, all right. Hold on. I'm coming." JP laughed despite the situation, "I'm coming, the Americans are funny people."

The ordering voice belonged to Agent Lewis, a tall, looming figure with a lean but muscular body and brunette hair. He wasn't alone. There were at least a dozen men with him. As Jean

Pierre opened the door, he thought he had caught a glimpse of Bilac. To his relief, the FBI agents didn't resort to forceful tactics like throwing him to the floor and handcuffing him. Instead, they calmly spoke to him, urging him to comply

Jean Pierre remained silent after changing into a blue shirt, black Dockers, and slacks. An evening suit was added to complete the ensemble. Within the tiny contingent of FBI agents that entered his room, he spotted Dumby among them. They bombarded him with peculiar questions and unsettling statements, claiming he was no longer the President of the United States. He immediately called out for Dumby, "Ted, hey, Dumby, hello? Mr. Congressman Ted Dumby."

Dumby looked up from the stack of papers and smiled at Jean Pierre. He mouthed a hello to him.

"What is going on, Dumby? Can you even hear me?" Jean Pierre sounded desperate.

Dumby ignored him and walked away.

Agent Lewis and his Captain, Captain Milford, and their team were all on standby, waiting for Jean Pierre to leave the room himself. If he kept sitting on the bed for another five minutes, they would hang him by his armpits, onto their shoulders, and throw him out of the third-floor room.

Jean Pierre slowly got up and saw Bilac, "Jerry, I mean Vice President Bilac, it is so nice to see you."

Bilac pretended not to know the ex-president that well. "Me?" He pointed to himself.

"Yes, oui, oui c'est moi, Jean Pierre, your friend."

"Let's not exaggerate, Mr. Labaguette. You hardly let

anyone come close but that friend from Haiti." Bilac picked up the pace and disappeared like a magician.

"Qu'est-ce que tu veux dire?[65] You don't know me?"

"He does, but perhaps not as well as you may have liked to think. Welcome to politics, Mr. Labaguette. Shall I say I hope you enjoyed your stay? This is when we, you and I, you and all of America, go separate ways." Agent Lewis said.

Jean Pierre looks at Agent Lewis, then at Captain Milford. "What happens now?"

"What do you mean? You took a dump on a country, and you're asking what happened?" Milford was beginning to lose his cool.

"No, no, I mean, how to say it? What will happen now?"

"Oh, you mean, 'what happens now'?"

"Oui."

"English, Mr. Labaguette, English, this is not France. It isn't even close to fucking Europe. Now get your ass up before I ask my men to... Before I relieve my men of all protocol, let them treat you like any other high-profile catch." Milford took a gander at JP with piercing eyes. "Do you understand, Mr. Jean Pierre Labaguette?"

"All right, man, take it easy."

"Go back to Auvers-Sur-Oise and skinny dipping in the Oise River."

JP smiled, "How nice, you know the names of my village."

---

[65] "What do you mean?"

"Also, the names, addresses, and contact numbers of all your friends and family and associates and...."

"No, you don't have that," JP replied, smiling at Agent Lewis.

"What do you mean?"

"You cannot tell the difference between conspirator and politician? Now, can you?"

"We do not have all day, Mr. Labaguette. Please hurry up."

"But you don't know all of them."

Lewis came close to JP and whispered in his ears, "When I said we know, I meant it. As for the Americans involved, they are sorted, but you? Not you nor your men in Cuba, London, or France. And once again."

"What?" JP raised his head to look up as he slowly rose from the bed.

"Welcome to politics, and we hope you enjoyed your stay." Captain Milford averted his gaze with a somber expression and exchanged words with Agent Lewis.

17

Marital Problem

"When a man steals your wife, there is no better revenge than to let him keep her."

— Sacha Guitry

The press and paparazzi were everywhere. They hounded any celebrity or political figure as though their lives depended upon it.

Such was the case with Sylvie. She was overtaken by lust. She could not control the feelings she had developed for the pool boy who was very well endowed and a great kisser, better than her husband, the ex-president, the tall, muscular boy wonder with black hair, who had won her emotional and sexual attachment.

Her husband and his career had taken a back seat in the list of her priorities; all she could see was her lover. The very sight of him blinded her. She would meet him privately and try to keep her association with him hidden from everyone's eyes, particularly that of her husband.

****

Nevertheless, Sylvie continued seeing Daniel, sometimes in hotels and others in an empty parking lot with the car's windows adequately tinted.

So, their relationship continued for quite some time. Sylvie often told him, "You are my pet, mon amour. I don't know how I spent my life before meeting you. You have made me feel all that Jean Pierre could never make me feel. Pleasure like never before."

Daniel responded, "You are love, ma Cherie. I would only have been an ordinary pool boy if it weren't for you. I feel as though you have raised my status and made me feel welcome in your life. My mind and body crave you. There is nothing that I wouldn't do for you. You name it, and it is yours, no matter the price. You may have my life, too."

Sylvie laughed. She had a sweet, silvery laugh. "You have already given me everything. I want nothing more except your fiery company and the joy and pleasure you give me. I feel intoxicated by your very presence."

She was aware that she was merely using him for her advantage. Moreover, she knew that if her husband ever discovered the truth, he would not hesitate to harm Daniel.

This person was none other than a press member who had been on their tail for quite some time, looking for hard-core evidence to reveal their iniquities.

He managed to take pictures of Daniel approaching a parked car in an empty parking lot. The vehicle was unmistakably Sylvie's car, and as Daniel opened the door, a press member quickly captured a picture of Sylvie's blond wig while her head was bent at an angle that obscured her face.

Nonetheless, the picture of her car showing the number plate and Sylvie's blonde hair was enough to uncover the matter and place the facts before the public. It was only apparent that Sylvie had tarnished her marriage and image, and Daniel, who had already lost his job as a pool boy, may now lose his life at the hands of Jean Pierre.

****

18

The Betrayal of His Haitian Friend

"Betrayal reveals hidden blessings; it removes toxic relationships to make space for better ones."

It was a fine afternoon when Fête Nationale asked Jean Pierre for an appointment to discuss business matters. JP conceded. When they sat down, Fête Nationale gave Jean a sly look and asked him, "How do you feel about the press breaking out about your wife?"

Pierre felt quite uncomfortable about this question and tried to waive it by saying, "Us politicians and other celebrities are always under scrutiny. They only saw a man enter my wife's car. There is nothing conclusive about that. I don't see why I should worry."

Fête Nationale gave Jean a pitiful look this time and said, "Well, you have every reason to worry. Because it was I who told the press where to find your wife and with whom. I left a margin of doubt on purpose. The paparazzi were told to take a shot, but that didn't clarify everything. But I tell you what, JP, it is a matter of just one move by me, and your whole reputation can come crumbling down. Just one move. "I have the bimbos to testify about our escape, and as you know, I paid them with your campaign money."

By this time, Jean Pierre was sitting upright, wondering what on earth Fête Nationale was saying. Finally, he looked across the table at Fête Nationale and said, "Come, my dear friend. How is it that you speak like a foe? I thought my secrets were safe with you. Why do you speak of exposing my wife and I?"

Fête Nationale laughed—a vicious laugh.

"You speak of friendship? There, there. You are a politician, after all. I thought you would be wise. Now see here." Fête Nationale leaned forward, lifted a briefcase on the ground next to him, and opened it. He pulled out a stack of photographs and threw them across the table at Jean. Jean stared as he realized the subject of these pictures was Sylvie's intimate relationship with Daniel and him in the VIP room Jean Pierre was taken aback.

He didn't know what to be more shocked about. His wife's betrayal, or the betrayal of his Haitian friend.

Jean Pierre found himself speechless and overwhelmed with

stress, desperately hoping that it was all just a nightmare as he rubbed his eyes. However, he knew it was a harsh reality. His anger began to rise, and he abruptly stood up from the table, with Fête Nationale following suit.

"So, tell me now, Jean Pierre, are you willing to part what is most dear to you? Or would you like me to hand these pictures over to the press? It can only take a day or so for the news to be out, and then your tenure as a politician would be over. I hope I am making myself quite clear here as to what is at stake if you refuse?"

By now, Jean Pierre had concluded that he would not die like a coward. Instead, he would face this with his head held high. So, he gruffly asked, "Fête Nationale, what is it that you want? And how can you assure me that after fulfilling your wishes, your mouth will indeed be shut?"

Fête Nationale laughed again, "Your restaurants are very lucrative and bring home a large income. How about you learn to part with them and give me the reigns."

JP was aghast, "What? Do you want to take over my restaurants? How can you come up with such a malicious plan? Is it unclear how hard I have worked to bring these restaurants to what they are today? I should've known better than to trust a scum-bug like you."

"Come, now. Giving these speeches about friendship and trust is not going to do you any good at this time. That ship has sailed. It is now time to talk about money. And about the restaurants. See, I will take over the restaurants, and in return, I will surely give you a small sum. I am not that hard-hearted. I will pay you some of your dues; the rest of the worth lies in these pictures. Now the ball is in your court. Take it or leave it. Say goodbye to your reputation if you choose not to part with your restaurants. The choice is yours."

Fête Nationale, gave him three days to consider his choices, warning that the compromising photographs would be given to the press if Jean Pierre didn't comply. For two days, Jean Pierre weighed his options, but eventually, feeling defeated, he let go of his restaurants.

He felt the bitterness of his political journey, leaving him a defeated man. He faced betrayal from both his political supporters in the Republican Party and the voters. He accepted that Americans might never truly become culinary connoisseurs, and the American way of life would remain the same. To add to his troubles, his wife preferred a younger lover. She became a vegetarian but worst of all gave up wine. Even his children underwent identity crisis, and his once-loyal ally, Fête Nationale Nationale, betrayed him.

19

House Arrest

"We the people are the rightful masters of both Congress and the courts, not to overthrow the Constitution but to overthrow the men who pervert the Constitution."

—Abraham Lincoln

Captain Humbert Livingston sat down with JP and delivered the unsettling news, "I am sorry that I had to take your brother out of prison, and now I must place you under arrest."

He fitted JP with an electronic monitoring device on his ankle, tracking his movements and location in the White House.

Feeling unjustly treated, JP demanded a lawyer and questioned whether he had committed a crime.

In distress, JP tried to remove the bracelet, but Humbert calmly explained, "I am just following orders, nothing personal. The Congress has initiated an impeachment process."

Handing JP a notification, Humbert cited Article One, Section 2, Clause 5 of the United States Constitution.

JP smiled and laughed, "Let me pardon myself." During Trump's closing days in office, he told aides he was considering pardoning himself." I can as well."

"I am sorry the president of the United States is constitutionally precluded from granting a pardon to impeached and convicted person(s)," Humbert replied, apologetic.

"The Constitution gives Congress the authority to impeach and remove "The President, Vice President, and all civil Officers of the United States" upon a determination that such officers have engaged in treason, bribery, or other high crimes and misdemeanors. "You are accused of treason of our way of life, colluding with foreign governments selling Louisiana to France, Alaska to Russia, participating in secret talks to the Canadian separatist, and organizing a coup d'état in Haiti..."

"And it seems you did not pay your taxes on your restaurants." Humbert further added, "I need your passport."

With reluctance, JP approached his desk and handed over his US passport. "

"What is that other passport you have? "

"My expired French passport. Do you have any authority to

take my French passport? It is expired anyway."

"Keep it. I have no instructions to hold it, but you are not authorized to leave the White House."

"White, Blue, and Red House, my friend. Let me call my lawyer."

****

In the following days, JP had several meetings with his lawyer, who happened to be a Jewish attorney with tinted hair and a strong Brooklyn accent. The lawyer had previously been associated with the Trump legal team but had distanced himself from the Republican party and avoided any indictments related to fake news.

The lawyer expressed the severity of JP's situation, stating, "Both parties are after you, and it doesn't look good."

He suggested negotiating a prisoner swap with France to serve time in jail, adding, "Perhaps you should talk to your brother; he might have some experience in this matter."

"The lawyer's forehead glistened with sweat, and traces of his black hair color began to smudge and ooze.

"Can't you fight for my freedom?"

"I can. Let me get back to you with a firm retainer figure. What $1,000,000 sound to you? "

"What it sounds to me is "like extortion and blackmail!"

"Think it over. Oh, and "one more thing," the lawyer added."

"What?" Jean Pierre asked.

"I can see some pastries on the table. Are they yours?" The lawyer's gaze fell on the table, where an assortment of meringues, almond petit fours, and a cherry clafouti was laid out.

"Yes, cooking saves my sanity."

With a slightly nervous chuckle, the lawyer asked, "Can I get one?"

"100,000 a piece, be my guest."

The lawyer's face quickly shifted from delight to disappointment. He hurriedly left the room without saying a word.

****

JP, under house arrest, took on the role of a chef for the Secret Service, and to their delight, they all savored his delicious creations.

As they relished the food, one of the Secret Service agents whispered, "I hope he stays on house arrest for a long time. Best food ever, what a talented guy!"

Amidst the appreciative comments, the clafoutis drew special admiration.

One of them raved, "His clafoutis are just heaven!"

Another chimed, "You've tried the cherry one, right?"

"Absolutely, and the pear one, too!" added John, an Asian American agent, enthusiastically.

20

Escape from the White House

"It is better to be alone than in bad company."

— **George Washington**

JP found himself on the "most wanted" list of international financial and political enemies he had made. Despite the electronic bracelet on his ankle, he remained under the close watch of the FBI.

Feeling that his only hope for sanity was to seek refuge with his brother in France, he decided to go into hiding. However, he still had access to confidential information and he identified a coyote group from Mexico. Without hesitation, he dialed one of the taped numbers, contemplating his next move carefully.

"Hello! Jorge?"

"Quién eres?

Jean Pierre put a handkerchief on the phone and spoke, "Mr. Jorge, I know everything about your smuggling operation, and I have all your phones tapped, but I can erase the information."

"Hijo the puta, Son of a "beach", Tendré una bala entre tus ojos y los ojos de los miembros de tu familia."[66]

JP replied, "I can do that as well. I know your wife, Angela, and your son, Pedro, who resides in Pasadena. "And you do not know who I am."

Jorge corrected himself, "Mr. President, my sound engineers identified your voice. You will never lose your French accent, will you? If you want to talk business, let's do it. From one head of state to another, are you still in charge? "I heard rumors of White House arrest.

"Jorge, I still have the power to erase your file. Will that work for you?"

"What may I do for your Mr. Ex-President?"

"I want you to smuggle a person across the border."

Jorge replied with a heavy silence.

---

[66] "Son of a bitch, Son of a beach, I'll have a bullet between your eyes and the eyes of your family members.

"Jorge, are you still there?"

"¿Estás bromeando? Are you joking, Mr. President? This is my daily living. Do you want to frame me?"

"No, sorry, I want you to smuggle a person out of the USA to Mexico."

"Consider it done, Mr. President. I will send you the instructions. But "who is the criminal to smuggle out?"

JP took a deep breath and replied, "It is not a criminal. I am innocent. It is me."

"You? Mr. President..."

"Yes, me."

"With your wife?"

"No."

"Your children?"

"No."

Jorge replied, "Mr. President, order some Tacos from the Mexican restaurant Taco Bill. Pide el especial Jorge...Order the Jorge special."

"I am sorry, Jorge, I need your help, but I do not eat Tacos."

"Mr. President, I do not want you to eat our food; the instructions will come in a Taco."

JP ordered the Jorge Special from Taco Bill in the following days. To maintain his cover, The President continued pretending to be depressed and suicidal. His sudden decision to stop cooking caused disarray among the Secret Service, who were accustomed to his culinary talents.

The house physician assessed his condition, remarking, "He is very depressed and delusional. He now craves Tacos and Mariachis. He's even shifted from French cuisine to Hamburgers, Hot dogs, and Soda pops. I'll put him on Prozac, but it will take a few days to work. In the meantime, let him have some Tacos and bring me some, too," he instructed the head of security.

The head of security replied, "But shall I inform my superiors?"

"No, my friend, Doctor order, do not bother. I am hungry. What about you?"

The head of the security's mouth watered with anticipation, saying, "Doctor's order, fine with me, I love Tacos."

The Mariachis entertained the President and the Secret Service as the meal arrived. The atmosphere was festive, but at one point, the President began to feel unwell. He was escorted to the restroom by the Secret Service.

While standing guard outside, the Secret Service agents could hear and smell some commotion and Montezuma's revenge from inside the bathroom. Trying to maintain their composure, they called out to the President, "If you need us, we are close by."

As time passed, no sound or smell came from the restroom, and growing concerned, they repeatedly called for the President, "Mr. President, are you okay?"

Worried, they finally called the house physician, who authorized them to force the restroom door open. To their astonishment, they found the President's ankle bracelet, a walkie-talkie, and an unconscious naked Mexican in the restroom."

"My God, this is not the President!"

"He escaped."

"The mariachis..." The head of security realized what had happened and immediately called security to block the gates.

JP sang in a van leaving the Blue White and Red House with the Mariachis, "Libertad, Libertad. "

Jorge had a minivan waiting for JP. They gave him a new phone, a freshly shaved face, and a complete transformation. They dressed him in women's clothes and a wig while they drove.

Examining his reflection in the mirror, JP expressed his dissatisfaction, "I don't look like a woman; I look like a man in women's clothes."

Antonio, a member of Jorge's team, sporting a Groucho Marx moustache and a beer belly, humorously replied, "Well, you look like a transgender person here. Here's your ID card, and if the police stop you, scream gender discrimination."

"We'll get you new clothes," Antonio continued, "Now, board a Greyhound bus to Laredo, Texas." He handed JP a paper and said, "Ask for Roberto at the hotel. They'll provide you with new clothes and a Mexican passport."

The Greyhound bus journey turned out to be monotonous, and JP felt the curious glances of fellow passengers. As if fate was playing its part, a transgender person entered the bus, beaming with a big smile. "Can I sit next to you, sister?" "His eyebrows raised. "Or shall I say, brother?"

They both chatted about politics, gender discrimination,

and the exorbitant cost of sex changes. JP added, "In France, it is free; the French Social Security pays for it. "

Michel, the transgender, started to call a few friends to tell them about the French Paradise for free sex changes. After kissing JP on the lips, Michel hopped out of the bus.

"Thanks, it was a sweet kiss that looked like a presidential kiss," he said as he winked, walking away on his high heels.

After traveling on several buses, JP finally arrived in Laredo without any police encounters and went to the Holiday Inn to meet Roberto, a tall man donning cowboy boots, jeans, and a sombrero.

"Hello, Mr. President," greeted Roberto, to which JP retorted, "Please, don't call me President, ever."

Despite his weariness, he was given food, new clothes, and a passport. Looking at the food with a hint of disdain, JP couldn't help but express his disappointment.

"Not really French cuisine," Roberto smiled, playfully moving his fork to the plate.

JP replied with a smirk, "Not really."

Roberto's comment inspired a thought, and JP humorously suggested, "Maybe you should teach us, with such a highly obese and diabetic population, how to eat better, Mexican style."

"Yes, it is needed," JP said as he took a bite.

"And maybe you could become our President," he said as he held himself against a chair to stop laughing.

"I get your point. No more President, please."

Accompanied by Roberto, JP crossed the Mexican border

from Laredo without hindrance. He asked about showing his passport at the border and expressed concern over his limited Spanish language skills.

Roberto assured him, "You don't need a passport in Mexico. You give money at the border to go in and out."

They crossed the border smoothly and proceeded on their journey. JP received a new phone and was driven to Cancun, where a cargo ship would take him to Dunkerque.

JP took over the galley and cooked for the crew during the trip, adding his culinary expertise to the voyage. The journey was enjoyable, filled with the melodies of Mexican music and the delicious taste of French cuisine, creating a harmonious blend of cultures as they sailed toward Dunkerque.

According to the captain, JP was a culinary gift from heaven. When they were a few miles from the harbor, the Captain called him and said, "Please take that." He handed him an envelope. "Take it to France. It will help you. Leave now before customs and immigration arrive. There is a small dinghy on the side. Ahmed will take you safely. France is heaven for migrants."

"I am not a migrant. I have an expired French passport."

"French...this is why you cook so good. It was the best journey I ever had."

Looking at the envelope, Jean Pierre whispered, "Captain, are these drugs? I have enough problems. I'm honest," JP asked.

The Captain reassured him, "No, this is just some cash for your cooking. You are welcome if you ever need another trip with us." As he shook JP's hand, tears welled up in his eyes.

JP boarded the dinghy with a small ladder, joining three other illegal immigrants already in the boat. They warmly greeted him, and during the journey, they excitedly discussed the benefits of France.

"You'll get free medical care," one of them exclaimed.

"And free housing, too!" added another. "France is the heaven of refugees."

"I am coming from El Salvador we cannot have tattoos anymore" added one of the Central American migrants.

Finally, they reached a small beach where a truck awaited them. Without hesitation, they hopped in."

21

Home Sweet Home – Return to His French Village

"If you could kick the person in the pants responsible for most of your trouble, you wouldn't sit for a month."

— **Theodore Roosevelt**

They left him at a train station, and from there he called his brother to tell him he was coming, his brother told him with joy in his voice that he had re married, JP boarded a train heading towards his village. As he looked out the window, the French landscape triggered a flood of memories.

The betrayals had deeply wounded JP.

His heart was shattered after the downfall of his political career, his wife's infidelity, his children identity crisis, his Haitian ex friend seizing control of his restaurants. He endured humiliation, house arrest, and legal prosecution. In the end, there was nothing left for him in the USA. Feeling utterly helpless and victimized, he couldn't bear to continue living a life of shame in the land of the braves.

He couldn't continue living a life of misery, not that things would be very rosy back in France. Nonetheless, JP thought of his family back home and thought reuniting with his brother would be a good idea to reminisce about old times. Realizing that his brother's adventure had been a well-orchestrated conspiracy, JP felt like they were both victims of the Americans.

He hired a cab at the train terminal.

He looked out the cab's window and felt the air brush across his face. At first, he felt quite at home until he realized that the village had changed drastically. Things were no longer well-lit, and the town had become a rather sultry affair. Not only had the weather changed, but it seemed the people had also changed.

"Vous venez de loin Monsieur?"[67]

"Des Etats-Unis"[68]

"Avez-vous suivit les nouvelles politiques?"[69]

---

[67] "Are you from far away, sir?"
[68] "From the United States."
[69] "Have you been following the political news?"

"Non la politique ne m'intéresse pas."[70]

"C'est dommage car les Etats Unis on fait une révolution politique."[71]

"Laquelle."[72]

"Ils remplacent les futures Président et vice Président par un programme d'Intelligence Artificielle."[73]

"Vraiment!"[74]

"Heureusement cela n'arrivera jamais en France."[75]

JP took a deep breath and looked outside as the taxi slowed down.

People did not seem to look at each other in the street, and the friendly atmosphere the village used to exude dissipated. Everything fell into a humdrum pace, and the area was no longer colorful. He felt as if he was in another world.

JP couldn't help but wonder what had caused such a drastic change in the village.

As he directed the cab driver towards his brother home, he eagerly looked forward to reuniting with his brother and his family, who was now re-married. They were expecting him, and he was excited to spend time with them.

---

[70] "No, I'm not interested in politics."

[71] "That's a pity, because the United States has undergone a political revolution."

[72] "Which one?"

[73] "They're replacing future Presidents and Vice-Presidents with an Artificial Intelligence program."

[74] "Really!"

[75] "Fortunately, that won't happen in France."

Upon reaching their house, JP was greeted at the door by his brother, PJ, who ushered him inside and introduced him to his wife, Fatima. JP couldn't help but notice that Fatima had a shy smile and wore a cloth wrapped around her head. He speculated that perhaps she had been in the kitchen and used the fabric to protect her hair... However, he also became aware that Fatima's head covering might be part of a Muslim faith, and he felt uncertain about the dynamics at play.

Nonetheless, JP decided not to address it immediately, as he wanted to understand the situation better and get a clearer picture of what was happening with his brother.

PJ seemed to have developed a mysterious air of peace and was sublimely unconcerned with the harsh realities of life in the village. The more JP talked to PJ, the more he realized that his brother had drifted off to another way of thinking and another state of mind altogether. He did not seem bothered by the seemingly minute things of life and often used words such as 'Masha'Allah,' 'Bismillah,' or 'Alhamdulillah.'

JP barely knew what these words meant and wondered if his brother was learning a new language. JP did not confront his brother but was beginning to develop an understanding that his brother had perhaps accepted Islam. JP began to feel uncomfortable but had no idea how to resolve the matter with PJ without being offensive.

After a while, JP felt he wanted some fresh air and wanted to visit the locality and see how things had changed in the area. So, he asked PJ if they could step out, to which his brother conceded. The two of them stepped out. They walked for some distance when JP noticed that the Church near their house was completely reconstructed and had several minarets.

215

This was indeed a Masjid, i.e., a Muslim place of worship. Once again, taken aback by his surroundings, JP couldn't contain his curiosity, so he finally asked PJ what was happening. PJ looked at him, puzzled, not fully grasping the question.

Sensing his brother's confusion, JP inquired, "Is this a Masjid? And I am not sure what you are doing with your life?"

The absence of women in the streets and the sight of numerous bearded men in Muslim attire shocked JP, especially considering he had only been away for ten years.

However, PJ seemed unfazed by JP's disapproval of the changes and took his comments lightly. He remained composed and unshaken, confident in his beliefs and choices. With a brief nod, PJ suggested they continue walking as he had something to show his brother.

Soon, they arrived at a sizable local restaurant prominently displayed Indian and Pakistani influences.

JP looked at it and said, "What the fuck is that? What is it?"

PJ responded as though he was stating, "I opened a Kebab Outlet, and I have converted."

JP was flabbergasted. He was at a loss for words. He did not know how to respond to his brother and resigned himself to silence lest he would offend PJ or hurt his feelings. Little did he know that PJ was above that. His new faith kept him happy, and he didn't need to prove anything to anyone.

PJ asked JP to accompany him inside the restaurant where they could sit and talk some more over some savory snacks before they went home to eat a meal prepared by his wife.

The restaurant was a quaint little place where people sat on low tables. On one side was a carpeted area where some people had spread what PJ later explained were called 'dastarkhwans.' As those people sat on the floor and ate, one could see that they were very comfortable and content with the setup.

As soon as they sat on the carpets, JP called the waiter, "A cognac, please."

The waiter looked aghast and immediately said, "Sorry, we do not serve alcohol here."

JP was losing patience with his brother by this time. "What have you done? Are you a Muslim? You have a kebab store? You do not drink alcohol?"

Then he looked around and said sadly, "At least you have a job. I have nothing, no wife, no money, and my children are with their mother and her lover." "My position has been terminated, I am the last US president, they have replaced Presidency and Vice Presidency by AI."

PJ took pity on JP and responded, "I am not working either."

JP impulsively asked, "Who is managing the restaurant?"

"My wife's brother."

"And you?"

"I am unemployed with four children. I make more money unemployed."

"So, what do you do all day?"

"I study The Quran and pray five times a day."

"This is crazy; you have changed your way of life, your identity. There is nothing French in you."

"After Macron, there's nothing French in the French either."

Then Pierre Jean broke down and said, "I will not exaggerate. I still smoke, I still go to see the prostitutes, and I participate in all the strikes."

****